PENGUIN BOOKS

other stories and other stories

Ali Smith was born in Inverness in 1962 and lives in Cambridge.
She is the author of *Free Love, Like, Other Stories and Other
Stories, Hotel World* and *The Whole Story and Other Stories*.

D1381657

04409095

ali smith

other stories and other stories

PENGUIN BOOKS

PENGUIN BOOKS

Published by the Penguin Group
Penguin Books Ltd, 80 Strand, London WC2R 0RL, England
Penguin Group (USA), Inc., 375 Hudson Street, New York, New York 10014, USA
Penguin Books Australia Ltd, 250 Camberwell Road, Camberwell, Victoria 3124, Australia
Penguin Books Canada Ltd, 10 Alcorn Avenue, Toronto, Ontario, Canada M4V 3B2
Penguin Books India (P) Ltd, 11 Community Centre, Panchsheel Park, New Delhi – 110 017, India
Penguin Group (NZ), Cnr Airborne and Rosedale Roads, Albany, Auckland 1310, New Zealand
Penguin Books (South Africa) (Pty) Ltd, 24 Sturdee Avenue, Rosebank 2196, South Africa

Penguin Books Ltd, Registered Offices: 80 Strand, London WC2R 0RL, England

www.penguin.com

First published by Granta Books 1999
Published in Penguin Books 2004
007

Copyright © Ali Smith, 1999
All rights reserved

The moral right of the author has been asserted

Every effort has been made to trace the copyright holders of the illustations and we apologize
in advance for any unintentional omission. We would be pleased to insert the appropriate
acknowledgement in any subsequent edition

Set in 12/14.5 pt Monotype Sabon
Typeset by Rowland Phototypesetting Ltd, Bury St Edmunds, Suffolk
Printed in England by Clays Ltd, St Ives plc

ISBN-13: 978–0–141–01801–0
ISBN-10: 0–141–01801–1

www.greenpenguin.co.uk

acknowledgements and thanks

thanks to the following publications, where stories
from this collection have already appeared:
*Scotland on Sunday, Wild Women, Granta Shorts,
Ahead of its Time, The Scotsman.*

a huge thank you to the Scottish Arts Council and the
Canada Council for the 1997 Scottish/Canadian
Exchange Fellowship, an extraordinary gift of time and
place where lots of the stories published here began.
Many many thanks to Stephen Brown, and to all the
kind people I met in Canada, particularly at Trent
University, Ontario.

many thanks also to Eastern Arts, for a bursary that
helped me over some lean months.

thank you, Becky.

thank you, Xandra and Alexandra.
thank you, Kasia, and thank you, Catherine.

thank you, Sarah.

For Sarah Wood
above all others

and for Kasia Boddy
story-lover

contents

Everyone, real or invented,
deserves the open destiny of life.

Grace Paley

god's gift

There are so many things that you don't know about me now. For instance. Some neighbouring cat has been bringing me birds, dead or dying, for several days. When I got back from Athens there were six mangled dead birds, and various other dead things, waiting in the garden for me among the newly opening flowers; for several weeks now I have been unlocking the back door and finding the corpse of a bird or what's left of a bird. Or if there is nothing at the back door and I go down the path thinking to sun myself on the patch of lawn, chances are the lawn will be a mess of feathers, feathers and gashed bird.

For instance, I open the door to go into the garden this morning and there is another bird on the mat. This one is alive. It is on its back with its wings tucked in and its feet in the air, pretending to be dead, but its whole body shudders every time its heart gives a beat.

Whichever cat it is is clearly deeply in love with me

or my territory; not just birds but slugs and worms are dragged and mauled over my turf; I've found the chewed-to-spokes wingframes of what seem to have once been late spring butterflies, and even, halfway up the path one day, a slice of bread, the end-slice of a Hovis. I suppose this could have been a gift from something other than a cat, could have fallen out of a beak out of the sky into my garden, or out of an aeroplane, though the logic of that would be more complicated. I am naive, I know; it still amazes me when I think of the waste products of humans atomizing instantly as they're shot out of thousands of aeroplanes into the sky, nervy flying people's shit and urine exploding unseen above us into particles so tiny they almost don't exist, floating down towards us through all the clouds of all the heavens round all the world. On the aeroplane on the way back, again for instance, the toilet I went to flushed itself with such ferocity that quite a lot of air was sucked out of the small cabin with it; it could have been frightening. I wasn't frightened, I wasn't frightened on any of the flights, since you are only frightened of losing something if you've got something to lose. Not you: one. One is only frightened, etc.

I went to Greece for a holiday, for fun. It was a good idea. I went by myself, a present to myself. When I sat on the waterfront on the first day of my week there, barely ten minutes into my stay in the small town, my luggage round my feet and too many clothes on for the heat, with the noise behind me, the men calling at tourists in the more probable languages trying to get them to come and eat at their restaurants, I saw the writing painted all along the wall out to the lighthouse, some Greek words I couldn't understand and then the English words, love, and you.

I got back on Tuesday, late. On Wednesday I cleaned up the garden, collecting the dead birds on the blade of the spade and balancing them out ahead of me and into the dustbin. On Thursday I found another, a blue tit, a young one, left for me under a bush. I picked it up using a plastic bag, turning the bag inside out so I could get the bird inside it without having to touch it. It was new dead, only just dead, and waves of heat came off the bag into both my hands in the cold; it was quite a cold day, it had been raining and I'd been surprised by how very light and perfected a thing the dead bird was, lying there in the rubble that gathers under a bush, the aimless stones and clayey ground, and how finished, curled and empty it was, its colours so brilliant and its claws already folded and useless.

It's Friday today. Today's bird, still breathing at my feet, is a fledgling thrush; it's so young its feathers haven't settled yet, fluffed and awkward. I slide my hand into the gardening glove and pick it up as carefully as I can because I know, shock can kill a life. Its heartbeat quickens. Its eye watches me from inside the curve of the canvas glove, it watches me all the way into the house, through the hall and up the stairs. I open the window with one hand and inch my other hand out of the glove, leave the bird on the glove out of the sun on the edge of the window sill where no cats will be able to get at it. I stroke its back with a finger to soothe it. There are parent thrushes calling somewhere overhead; I can't see them but I recognize the noise, the panicked call for the loss, and know that they've been calling for well over an hour, that I heard that same call when I was lying in bed just wakened.

In the back garden half an hour later I can't stop thinking about the bird. It might be dead by now. But as far as I know it's all right, it is still alive at the front of the house on the sill, maybe twitching a leg or trying first tentative moves with its wings or bending its head round and opening a beak, soundless, to the sky where its parents are, where they're calling, I can hear them, and I have no way of telling them where it is.

It has a fifty–fifty chance, unless its back is broken. I haven't seen any blood or any obvious puncture marks. Then I come out in a cold sweat. I hope to God its back isn't broken. I touched it on the back. Perhaps I gave it pain. Perhaps I hurt it even more than it was already hurt.

Beyond the scraping call of the thrushes there is other insistent cheerful birdsong draping itself above the gardens, lacing itself in and out of the trees. The first girl I ever fell in love with put a bird in my bed. She did, yes, she did. That's something I'd forgotten and remembering it so suddenly makes me laugh out loud. She was a sweet love, a sweet lover, my first. I was her first too. Now when I think of her it can be with almost no regrets, with hardly a twinge of discomfort, with positive nostalgia, and it was a stuffed bird she put in my bed, I remember; it was supposed to be a joke. Her father collected them from auction rooms and taxidermists, stuffed owls and terns and things, and one night, the night before an important exam I had to sit, she came to see me for half an hour to wish me luck, left at ten o'clock, and when I went to bed four hours later with my head full of barely memorized formulae I found it tucked in under the covers with its head on my pillow and its pedestal jutting up through the bedclothes.

I'm laughing. I was angry and disgusted. I picked it up between two textbooks and held it at arm's length, carried it through and left it standing (like I suppose it still is standing somewhere, with its chest puffed out and its eyes glued into its head, with one leg fixed in place in front of the other and both feet stuck to the fake rock on the pedestal) on the floor of the shared kitchen of the hall of residence, and I went back to my room and changed the sheets swearing under my breath at two in the morning. I imagine my horrified face as I changed the sheets. I'm laughing so much now that one of the neighbours twitches her upstairs curtain, looking to see what the noise is. I'm laughing in my garden by myself for no reason on a Friday morning at half-past ten when people don't normally sit out in their gardens, when all normal people are somewhere at work.

I pretend I haven't seen her. I am doing something. I am reading a book. I am reading up about some of the places I importantly went to last week. I look down past the page and see that a greenfly has drowned in my coffee. I lift it out. Near my feet a bee is crawling on the ground under the bush where I found the dead bird yesterday, examining the fallen leaves for anything good to take. It's warm today, close. There are wakened insects everywhere. There are spiders running through the grass and in and out of cracks in the wall. A long blue something, like a blue-coloured stick, is holding on with its front legs to the end of a dead stalk. I wonder if it is a dragonfly. Out of the corner of my eye I notice a rosebush over there bristled with greenfly, as if the greenfly are growing on it like very small green fruits and the bush is thriving with them. I should spray them. Soapy water will do it.

Parthenon means virgin's apartment. I went there on Monday. There were tourists queuing up and taking photographs of each other in front of ancient things. I overheard a good-looking girl say in an American accent, this is what dying will be like, this is what arriving in heaven will be like, and I thought, she's right, hundreds and hundreds of people of all these ages and nationalities arriving together and queuing up and standing around looking at things, and some will be wearing cagoules, and some will be taking photos of their friends, and some will be drawing heaven in their sketchbooks, and some will be sitting down eating their packed lunches.

I had my lunch in a place called Dionysos's Restaurant, at the foot of the Acropolis. It's in the guidebook. *Try Dionysos's Restaurant, at the foot of the Acropolis – it may not be cheap, but you'll eat in*

style, and what's more, with the most important
remains of ancient civilisation as your personal view.
It's quite a good book, this guidebook. It tells you all
sorts of things, like how not to get ripped off by taxi
drivers, and how the real Caryatids are in the museum
and the women holding up that building with their
heads aren't the originals. It's got incidental things in
specially highlighted paragraphs about the Greek gods,
and about archaeology, things like how clay bulls
would be substituted for real bulls when people
couldn't afford a real bull for sacrifice and had to kill
something lesser. How the clay statues of goddesses,
their arms out in blessing or cupped in hopeful fruit-
fulness, and jewellery, valuables, pictures, portraits,
cups and trinkets, would be buried with the dead, and
the dead would have coins in their mouths, placed on
their tongues, to pay their passage to the underworld.
I saw rows and rows of those tongue coins in one of the
museums. I wonder now whether those particular dead
people won't have had their passage paid, will still be
standing blank-eyed at one side of the river waiting for
a boat that never comes, since their coins are in
museums now and not in their mouths any more.

In Chania most of the old town is still war-damaged,
though it's hard to tell which war. There are posh jewellery shops, coiffure shops, supermarkets and cafés all
on the ground floors of buildings that are open ruins
upstairs. Thin cats run wild up and down and through
the crumbling houses that have no roofs; grass and
flowers grow on the ledges of windows that reveal their

insides as nothing but sky. For instance one evening I ate on the stylish upper floor of a ruin, three floors of which were decked out with tables and chairs. The waiter liked my sunglasses. He kept trying them on and going off to show his friends, the other waiters, what he looked like. Above our heads, infinity; swallows screeching, diving low then high in spacious dangerous figures of eight.

I am Adonis, the waiter said, sitting down at my table after he'd finished bringing me things to eat. It was late, it was dark; there was hardly anybody else in the restaurant. He had brought free brandy, had put it down with a flourish on the table and slid himself into the seat opposite.

No, he said, it is not funny, it is true, it is my real name. You are sad. I will help you. We are friends. This is for you. It is five stars. Your glasses, I like them. When you get back to England, you will send me glasses like these.

He was small and tanned, handsome and weasly at the same time, and he filled my brandy glass five times to try and get my sunglasses, but I kept them. I went home with the cook in the end; she and I had been watching each other over the steaming grill all evening. She was short and dark and pretty, and greasy from work, and neither of us spoke a language the other could understand; when I swayed my way down the rough stones that were once the staircase of a house, Adonis behind me calling me to come back and sit down, she was waiting for me wordlessly at the foot of

them. I have no idea how we made it through the blur
of backstreets to my apartment with its smell of damp
animal fur, but we did, and I think we made love, I'm
pretty sure we did, though what I remember more
clearly is that I was sick afterwards in the sink, and in
the morning I woke up and Elena (I think that was her
name) was scooping grease, bits of meat, little bits of
rice, what was left of my insides, out of the sink into
the toothbrush glass and pouring it into a carrier bag.

I apologized and she understood and smiled and said
something, turning back to the sink. I could hear the
church bell beyond the shutters, ringing, six. When
she'd finished she tied a knot in the top of the carrier
bag and left it by the pipes underneath, washed her
hands in the clean sink, dried them on my towel and
then she left. The sun was up. I went back to sleep,
woke to a shaking hangover, and that's what I
remember of last week, really. Ruins, and kindness.

I'm dying, you said to me once, one time when you
were feeling sick.

No you aren't. Don't be stupid, I said. I felt your
temperature. You seemed all right.

No, you said, I am, my stomach really hurts, I'm
dying of illness.

I got you Pepto Bismol from the bathroom cabinet
and tucked you into bed with the covers up round your
chin, and you were fine, I was right.

Because I know, I know, I know. I know every day,
every hour is a gift. I know, yes, every moment, even
these ones, this one, now, here on this derelict lawn.

I know all that, I always knew it, and I am trying to remember it, each small flurry of wings above a rubbly back garden, each infinitesimal hope. Everything you do, everything you see, everything you feel, every single moment, good or bad, that you get. Not you: one. Every single moment, good or bad, that one gets.

I open my eyes. The birdsong is continuous. Clouds have massed in over the houses; the birds are singing in that echoing way that promises rain and I can't hear the thrushes any more with their scratchy lament. That means one of two things.

In a moment I will go upstairs and see if the fledgling is still on the glove on the window sill. If I can see a bird still there, then it's probably dead. If I can't see a bird on the sill, then it's probably alive. But it might have fallen off, or been blown off. What if it fell off? It might have fallen the height of the house and be stunned or killed on the ground below.

If there is no bird on the sill what I will do is this. I will go to the window and lean out. I will look down, and it will be there. Or I will look down and it'll be gone.

It will be dead.

It will have flown.

the hanging girl

They're going to hang me.

I don't think they will blindfold me. The sun on the snow. What a day, a beautiful spring day. Smell of sawn wood. One of the men is holding the ropes. Not men, boys. Another hits at my feet with his gloves and shouts something over his shoulder. I think they think I am too near the edge. They don't want me to hang myself. Clean wood underfoot. I think everyone from the house is already dead. They are doing this to other people too. I don't recognize any of them. My wrists have made the ends of my sweater loose and round and the cold air gets in. I haven't changed my clothes for six days. The rope round my wrists is hairy. Not too tight. Just tight enough. The boy who tied them was kind. They've made signs to hang round our necks. The signs have two languages on them. What I can read says we have been made an example of. Spring is coming. When they took me out there were chickens pecking in the snow where the snow is thinner, and there is a crow somewhere in the trees, the noise of a crow. The way crows build their nests, balanced on nothing, on the holes between branches.

A man is pulling pointed legs out from beneath a camera. I don't know what type of camera it is. It's a film camera. This will be filmed. People have sat down on the chairs to watch. Something is going to start soon. A man just got up and gave his chair to a lady. They are having a conversation. She's looking at the sky and nodding. The man with the greatcoat has stopped in front of me. His head comes up to my stomach. He's standing on something. I can't see what it is. I can't see his face. There's snow on the brim of his hat. It hasn't snowed for days. He must have come through trees. He is sliding the knot round away from my chin. The knot makes his hand in its glove look small. He has moved to the woman next to me. I think I can get myself to the edge again. The camera has started making a noise. Careful. Careful.

Here I go here I go here I go again the big number one more time ladies and gentlemen put your hands together please for this little lady a singer a swinger in the performance of a lifetime (music applause) start spreading the noose I'm leaving today slow slow build it build it up blast it out thank you thank you ladiesan-gentlemen I'm a little hoarse forgive me my throat's a little tight for it today but a very warm welcome to the show I'm your (g)host for this evening morning after-noon evening morning afternoon and I just know we're

going to have a really great time together why did the
chicken cross the road? well wouldn't you if someone
wanted to wring your neck? (groans of laughter) why
couldn't they hang the insolent girl? because she had
such a – yes – brass neck (laughter and clapping) no no
please no time for that a lot to get through no time to
hang about (laughter) yes! please! madam! thank you!
but to be serious just for a moment – only for a
moment sir don't look so worried! – in all seriousness
remember (dim lights to spot and cue grave music)
nothing that you will see tonight is faked *nothing* that
will pass before your eyes here is fabricated in any way
no tricks of the light no tricks of the lens this death is
pure live entertainment and I swear it will really
happen right before your eyes over and over and over
again for over and over amen boys girls ladies gentlemen thank you I appreciate it I do and now (drumroll)
the moment we're waiting for . . . today's victim on . . .
This Is My Death – yes it's you yes this time you now
from nowhere you get more much more than you
bargained for me you get me scrawny broken albatross
to hang round your neck in one lunge I'm off the scaffold and into your head surprise! and swinging gaudy
bauble on a tree coo-ee hello it's me hung by my thread
first my face before the rope then my face tight pinched
constipated those tight lines are my eyes and mouth
halfway through the slow snap in two ah then my eyes
rolled to heaven a blank thank you thank you ladies and
gents ghastly I know so nice to meet you to make your
acquaintance nice knowing you pity it was so short but

no more time oh well never mind see you later alligator goodnight Irene I'll see you in your dreams.

My head at its broken angle. My eyes gone. The creak of the rope on the beam above.

Please, you boys in the front row. Please. No filming up my skirt.

Anyone like to see it one more time? Push button one for yes, button two for no.

Pauline went to the doctor's. I've got aches and pains all over, she said. I feel dizzy and light-headed. My stomach's sore after I eat. My skin feels sensitive like I've got flu, and I'm having delusions.

Delusions, the doctor said.

I keep imagining there's somebody behind me, but the thing is, there's nobody there, Pauline said.

Somebody behind you, the doctor said. He clicked the mouse on his computer.

Following me, Pauline said. All the time. Wherever I go. But every time I look round, whoever it is is gone.

Mm, the doctor said. Interesting.

It's very disconcerting, Pauline said. Actually it's getting to be a bit of a pain in the neck.

Where exactly in the neck? the doctor asked.

Not just the neck, all over really, Pauline said. Can you give me an antibiotic?

The doctor printed out a prescription. Take the whole course, he said. I think the unspecific aches will clear up. It's probably what we call a rota bug. You need some indigestion tablets for the stomach. You might find it cheaper to ask at Boots for their own name brand, they're just as good. As for the other, I'll refer you to our counsellor.

Thanks, Pauline said.

It took three months for Pauline's referral. By the time she was sitting in one of the plush armchairs on the other side of the desk from the counsellor she had lost a substantial amount of weight, there were black circles round her eyes, and her hair had outgrown the style it was supposed to have.

It's a woman, she whispered, a woman or a girl, I can't tell which. I can only just catch her, and only sometimes, in the corner of my eye. I'm pretty sure she's here now. I don't really like talking about her in the third person. It seems rude.

Behind the counsellor's head there was a poster of the Munch painting of the screaming person on the bridge. Above the face was the word DEPRESSION and a question mark, in shimmery out-of-focus letters.

The piece of plastic on her desk said that the counsellor's name was Mrs Jane Figgis. Mrs Figgis looked tired. She wrote down Pauline's name. Now then, she said. Pauline. We've got a six-week block of meetings, Pauline, and I'm hoping you will be able to make it here to the office at this time every week for the next five weeks not including today.

I will, Pauline said.

Including this week, that makes six weeks in all, Mrs Figgis said. Now. If you feel like you're going to be unable to keep to this arrangement, for any reason at all, for instance if you're ill, or you have another appointment somewhere else, or you just don't feel like coming, if you could telephone reception and explain that you can't comply with our schedule on that particular week.

Yes of course, Pauline said, but I'm always available on Thursday mornings, Thursday's fine for me.

Because if you cancel, Pauline, you see, you must understand. Whether you choose to or you have to forego one of our scheduled meetings, regardless of reasons I'm afraid, you'll lose that meeting altogether. I just have to make that clear, and I hope it isn't a problem for you, Mrs Figgis said.

No, no problem at all, I understand, Pauline said. She signalled with her eyes to the armchair on the left of her. She's here now, she said. I think she's in that chair there.

Yes, the counsellor said. She wrote something down and looked at her watch. Tell me about yourself, she said. Let's start with your childhood.

It's nothing to do with my childhood. When I try to picture it, the entity called childhood, it repeats on me, rich and well-meaning as a glass of milk and I know that it was a time of effortless seasons, fanning down one after the other like the pages of a book slow-riffled by the thumb of some blithe, indolent hand.

My name is Pauline Gaitskill. I was born in July 1966. I work for Hummings Mints; I design the combinations of sugar, flavouring and chemicals to make the

insides of the Hummings range chewy and harmless.
I've been doing this for the six years since I left college.
I'm solely responsible for several things: Hummings
Chewy Spearmints, Hummings Chewy Peppermints
and Hummings Chewy Strongmints. At the moment I
am working on a potential new project, Hummings
Chewy Traditional Olde English Mints.

Recently something has changed for me. It is possible, I suppose, that it's been changed for longer, that
I just didn't notice, but I've been aware of it since the
first week of November last year.

I remember because that night we had friends over;
we had stripped our front and back rooms and we
were celebrating our new polished wood floor. Our
friends brought some dope, which made us hilarious
and we were lolling and giggling round the aftermath
of supper. The table was strewn with our leftovers.
Someone had left the television on in the adjoining
room, a programme where some elderly people
were talking about their lives, and every so often, I
remember, there would be film of mounds of dead
bodies from all over the world over the century, over
the lifetimes of the old people. The thing I remember
is that every time any one of us caught sight of these
dead bodies in the other room we would all end up
destroyed, in helpless laughter.

Mike is my partner. He makes toothpaste dispensers;
we're perfectly suited. That night he was telling Roger
and Liz about something he'd read in the Sunday
paper, where the last words of pilots in planes about to

crash were recorded, and were usually oh fuck or oh
shit or oh Christ. Then we all joined in making up
people's famous last words. Marc Bolan: at least I went
out on a smash hit. Marie-Antoinette: did you have to
take so much off? I only wanted a trim. (I thought that
one up.) Liz had one about Princess Diana, I don't
remember. I remember we had a long and detailed argument about whether famous last words were valid after
or before the death, and we eventually decided that
they'd have to be said before to count, since you
couldn't really say anything after you were dead, and
then we went round the table and each of us had to
think of one. Look how close I can get to the edge of
this cli-i-i-i-. Do you think we should be driving quite
so fa-. Don't worry, it's perfectly sa-. Liz had one
which was the same each time with different endings.
Why are you coming towards me in that threatening
way with such a big sharp kitchen kni-, that tennis ra-,
hypodermic syri-, sawn-off sho-. There were people
lining up in black and white on television, about to be
shot or hung. I pretended to be one of them. I said: I
really wish this was just a game of famous last wo-. I
got the biggest laugh. We were laughing our heads off.

The next day my head felt all light. The next day
was the first day I had an inkling that something might
actually be wrong.

The waiting room was full of people waiting to talk to
counsellors. Pauline stood at the receptionist's desk
until the receptionist looked up from her screen.

I won't be coming to my appointment next week, Pauline said. Or the week after that, or, I'm afraid, the week after that. And I won't be able to come next month at all. I'm very busy next month.

The receptionist clicked up the first of Pauline's appointments and began deleting the letters of her name. Pauline pushed through the heavy swing doors. She paused to hold the door open. She didn't want it to swing back and hit whoever was at her heels.

Pretty blonde Pauline turning heads in the sun of a June afternoon. Blonde and wide-eyed like a girl from an old-fashioned hairspray commercial, frowning slightly, quite attractively, as if concentrating; looking all the better for being a little too gaunt; her long hair shimmering and the sight of her sending a pleasant shiver over the surfaces of the hearts of passers-by as she walked down the street.

Pauline stopped suddenly, very suddenly turned round.

Nearly, she said in a whisper. Nearly caught you.

Pauline talking to the ghost as she walked, but quietly so nobody would think her deranged, humming what she said into a singsong so anybody would think her just strolling along, singing a song. Me and my sha-dow, strolling down the a-ven-ue, me and my sha-dow. I know you're there. What do you want. I know you want something. What do you want from me. She smiled back at a man who was smiling at her from behind his fruit stall.

Day-dreaming, darling?

Yes, I suppose I am, she said.

Can I do you anything today, love?

Not today, thanks.

Pauline went into an empty church, sat down at the back.

Is this right? she said under her breath. Is this any good?

The church was shockingly cold. Pauline sat in a pew then lay down on her back. She looked up at the rafters. A medieval-looking man hung carved into the wall. He had his arm round the shoulder of another man most of whose face had been chiselled off, and he was holding open the wound in his own side so the man with no face could put his fingers into it. The face that remained was patient, indifferent. Pauline sneezed, and heard the sneeze repeat itself in the church a fraction of a second after it had left her nose.

Bless me, she said.

Less me, the echo said.

She lay as flat as she could. She crushed out the space between her back and the wood she was lying on.

Nothing there, she said.

Air, the echo said.

I give up. I'm going mad. I am, Pauline said.

Vup. Ad. Am, the echo said.

Out on the street heat haze or car haze hung at the traffic lights. Pauline crossed the road to the fruit stall and bought eight oranges from the man.

Got a cold? the man said.

Vitamins, Pauline said.

At the newsagent's she bought a newspaper and a bottle of water. When she came out she saw the girl hanging from a lamppost. She watched her, cut down, fall through the air and crumple on to the ground.

The bottle smashed open on the pavement. The oranges rolled into the road. A boy stopped his bike and picked up what he could as the cars roared past. He held out his arms full of oranges to the woman standing with her mouth open, broken glass round her feet and water seeping into the cracks in the concrete. A mother tugged on a small child's hand, told her to come away.

Are you in pain? Pauline said.

Eh? the boy holding the oranges said. You all right? All right then?

The women watching from the pelican crossing decided between them that she was drunk.

Your poor head. Is it heavy? Pauline said.

The water was evaporating already on the pavement. The boy put the oranges down, stepped back.

She draped the hanged girl's arms round her shoulders, hoisted her on to her back. The girl's head swung down, loose, hung round Pauline's neck. Pauline held it in her bare hands.

I think we are friends now. She is much less shy than she was to start with, and I have invited her to stay for as long as she wants. She is staying in the guest room. I have been trying to explain to Mike, but he just refuses to see it.

She has an endless appetite for television. She lies on the couch with her head propped on the arm of it and watches tv like a sick child. (Actually I think she only is about twelve, or thirteen at the most.) She loves quizzes, game shows, shows where people sing. She particularly seems to love old musicals. She watched the whole of *Oliver!* and I could tell, she was moved, especially when Nancy gets killed.

She becomes quite agitated if anything serious is on. Mike gets very angry and we have had several arguments, the last and most furious so far over a documentary film of some Canadian loggers taking chainsaws to trees. But she didn't want to see it and I will not have her suffer. Anyway Mike didn't really want to watch it; he's never wanted to watch such things before. He was just trying to prove a point.

For someone with such bad co-ordination she gets around pretty well. She likes to hang herself from things all over the house. She's tried out all the light fittings in all the rooms. She likes the upstairs banister rail; she enjoys the drop in the landing. Last night she hung on the wall like a picture. I think she was trying to make me laugh.

It is exciting having a friend again. Mike is a little resentful, which is unreasonable. It's not as if we skulk in corners and discuss him or anything. It's not as if we talk at all. I don't believe she understands English, even if she could talk. I sing to her sometimes; it's a universal language. I show her words in the paper and try to explain them until she looks bored. We have a book of photographs of wild flowers. She is always signalling to me to find the pictures of the small pink ones, field bindweed, and the small blue ones, forget-me-not.

The way her eyes are set up beneath the lids makes her look cynical, and once you get to know her she's not like that at all. She hangs off the tree at the bottom of the lawn and birds swoop round her, rest on her shoulders or the side of her head. One day I lay on the grass and she lay beside me; we stayed there all afternoon and all evening, until it got dark. She wanted to watch the things coming out of the ground.

I would like to remove what's left of the rope. It looks heavy and uncomfortable; it must rub. But when I showed her the knife – it's too thick for scissors – she flew off up the stairs in a panic and hung from the light in the back bedroom and wouldn't come down. I heard her thump back on to the carpet well after I went to bed.

I wonder what her name is. I have no idea how to find out. I tell her, to comfort her, because she must need comfort, that there's nothing so strange or different about it, that she's missing nothing, that it's the same for everyone; every one of us falling through air with one end of the rope attached to our birthdates till the rope pulls tight. Some people just have less far to fall, I say.

But she looks at me with her white eyes, her head hanging like an empty ventriloquist's dummy, and I know what the look means. Some people are pushed. Some people aren't given enough rope. You can't know what it was like.

True. I don't know. I have no idea what it was like.

I can make a good guess as to where she is now. In her favourite place, doing her favourite thing, swinging beneath my kitchen clock pretending to be the pendulum.

Pauline stopped going in to work. Mike found out when Pauline's boss called his office to ask if she was any better. He drove home in the middle of the day and found her lying on her back on the lawn, staring at the sky with her hair in the soil beneath the rose bush.

That night in bed he put his head on her arm.

Love, he said. Baffling, all this. Really it is.

No, Pauline said. Baffling is where they hang you by the foot; they used to do it in parts of Europe and in Scotland, it's a symbolic sacrifice, like putting you in the stocks. They did it to people who owed money or to perpetrators of mild forms of treason. It's not the same thing at all.

Mike sat up, took Pauline by an earnest hand, made his face earnest. Tell me it again, he said. I'm trying to understand. In your dreams, and in your head –

– uh huh, in my dreams, if you like, Pauline said

– you've got this pretty girl always going to her death, Mike said.

A pretty girl going to her death, Pauline said. Does the prettiness make a difference?

Of course, Mike said. He smiled. I'd think it'd be much harder to watch a pretty girl having to die, he said.

Pretty, Pauline said. Well, it's hard to tell. She's beautiful, of course. But it's not what you'd call a pretty sight. But yes, I suppose she was once pretty. Or she might have been, if she'd had the chance. Anyway, she's a friend. Friends are always pretty, even if they're not.

Pauline stared at the wall. Mike lay back and watched her stare into space. He thought about the three thin pretty girls from the American sitcom about friends, and then he imagined them on their way to die. He made up various possible deaths for them. Then he replaced them with some of the prettier girls from work.

Christ, he said.

He turned over so Pauline wouldn't sense his erection, closed his eyes and shook his head sharply, pictured himself instead, driving along the motorway under turn-off signs and signs flashing warnings about fog, driving fast along boring country lanes and slowing as he came into a village, past a sign about old people crossing, a sign about a hump-backed bridge, a narrowing of the road, a sharp bend, a sign saying keep your distance.

I don't know what to do, Mike told Roger at lunch. I'm at the end of my tether. She won't go to work. She won't answer the phone. She won't come out, not even down to the pub for a quick drink. She sits in the house all day in a room with the curtains closed, or on the kitchen floor with her legs crossed leaning against the fridge, or she shuts herself in the bathroom and talks to herself. She won't talk to me. She watches rubbish all the time on tv. Her work phoned me; they can't sign her off sick without a sick note and she won't go to the doctor, she keeps saying she's better. But she lies in bed all day and won't get up. She's hardly eating. I've bought her presents. They make no difference.

Yeah, Roger said. Liz says she can't get her to speak to her. She says it's as if she's a different person. She thinks she needs therapy.

She's been, Mike said. She won't go back. The therapist told her it was displaced guilt.

What's this? Maggie said across the table. What's this about guilt? Somebody's guilty of something around here and I don't know about it?

Mike bristled. He didn't want anyone else listening in.

Pauline says it's a load of rot, he said to Roger. She says there's nothing displaced about it and the sooner we all realize it, the better.

Yeah, right, Roger said. He frowned. Guilty of what? he said. He hadn't really been listening, and didn't want Mike to realize. He began wondering whether Pauline was having an affair after all, like Liz thought. (He and Liz had been discussing it. In fact they had had rather a nice time discussing it, and had gone out for a meal specifically to do so, and had spent more time talking to each other because of it than they had for quite a long time, and afterwards they had been exceptionally close and had had some very good sex.)

Well, you know, Mike said. Like when. Like this thing that happened about a month ago, I was reading this piece out of the paper about soldiers taking an amateur video of each other pretending to be shooting people in the mouth and raping people, and the paper had got hold of the videotape and now the soldiers were in trouble. I mean, it isn't even a *real* bad thing, but she went running crying out of the room. I mean, it was only them having a laugh. I told her. Terrible things happen all the time. You can't be this sensitive, you just can't.

No, Maggie said, you can't, can you? When Dave and I were in Washington we went to the museum they've got about the holocaust, you know? It's an amazing building. But it's so depressing, and it's really tiring.

Liz's father, Roger said, used to do this thing. He used to take pictures of gravestones all the time. Liz has all these photos of her and her mother and sisters on days out in cemeteries. Her father used to make them go because it was easy to park and you could always find somewhere to sit. Weird. I mean, sick.

Spooky, Maggie said looking at Mike.

Right, Mike said. He was sweating. He held his arms close in to his sides, in case there were patches showing under them. He looked at his plate, at what looked like gristle on his fork. Last night he had woken in the middle of the night from the same dream, the recurring dream, where his parents appeared to him smiling, vibrantly alive.

He glanced at Maggie, across from him, all sympathetic face. He could feel Roger looking at him, paused over his pudding, waiting to hear more, to find out what the trouble was. He looked at the clock. Lunch hour was almost up and he'd eaten hardly any lunch.

Inside his mouth he could feel his tongue, rooted to him like a thick-stemmed plant. It was moving. It touched against the soft flesh of the walls of his mouth.

You can hang a work of art. You can hang a whole exhibition of works of art. You hang meat until it properly matures, and a jury or a parliament can be hung.

You can hang on somebody, on his or her every word, and something can hang on, depend on, something or someone else. Clothes can hang well on you. Something can hang over you. There's the other kind of hangover. There's hang out and hang dog and get the hang of. Hang back. Hanging garden. Hang together. Hang down your head, hang fire, hanger on and hang on (as in, wait a minute). Hang in the balance. Well-hung. Hang-up (psychological), and hang up (telephone).

I have started to make lists of these into a kind of mantra to try to interest her, even if only subconsciously, in all the other possible meanings. It is the least I can do.

I touch my neck, apply different pressures to the cords of my muscles. It amazes me how tough and sensitive they are. I speak while I'm doing it, and hear how the pressure changes the sound that comes out.

I carry her up the stairs. I put her down on the bathroom stool, run the water, swirl the hot and the cold together. I dry my hands and undress her, as gently as I can because she is always sore. Then I lift her up and slide her into the water and she rests her head on the side of the bath. I soap her all over. Her feet, between her toes, up her calves and thighs and between them, up her taut back and down her front, between her ungrown breasts, under her arms, round and under the rope. I squeeze the flannel out over her head and wash off anything left of the soap. Then I wrap her in the bathtowel that's been warming on the radiator. I dry her all over. I dry between her toes and behind her knees with talcum powder. I towel her hair and comb it out. I carry her on my back into the bedroom, and then I tuck her into the bed. Until she is asleep, I lie next to her above the covers. She likes me to breathe with her. When she is asleep I slip off the bed, switch the light out and close the door over. I leave the landing light on. She is afraid of the dark.

On the nights when she can't sleep, I sit with her. I look into her white-charred eyes. I let her put her cold hand on my heart.

It is the very least I can do.

Pauline jumped off the garage roof and broke her leg when she landed. The bone came right out through the skin.

A neighbour called both the paramedics and the police for good measure. The policeman arrived first.

I can't help you, love, he told Pauline. I'm the reporting officer. Even if you were on fire, even if you were bleeding to death right here in front of me on the lawn, I'd not be able to do anything. It's my duty only to report what happens here until the emergency services come.

Pauline lay on the grass with her leg jutted up. Tears streamed across her face and she was laughing. The policeman looked at her teeth. He thought what a fine mouth she had, and how very good-looking she was. He turned his back, one foot swivelling in the flower-bed, opened his book and wrote it down. Upon my arrival the young woman was hysterical, and was quite unable to assess her own position.

Mike was round at Maggie's. He had been walking back and fore outside her house, and now he was sitting on her couch holding a large whisky. Maggie was saying all the right things; all the useful, surprisingly comforting things. But none of us can do anything about it, she said. We'd all like to, but we can't. However much we'd like to, it's just not possible. Some things are out of our control. We have to survive. She needs help, Michael, professional help, the kind of help you and I just can't give her.

Mike liked it that Maggie called him Michael. It somehow made things feel new, and possible.

Where's Dave? he said.

Not here, Maggie said.

Mike's head and throat felt tight, as if he were about to cry. Maggie, I'm scared, he said.

Don't be, Maggie said. Don't be scared.

She was behind him, and she leaned forward and

brushed her hand across the back of his neck, and where her hand touched him his hair stood on end.

She took me to a slightly higher place so we could see better.

She brought her friends. They crowded in to see, all their grey forms in a mass upon the lawn, they over-filled the garden and the other back gardens and crammed into the lanes, spilling across the road and down the road. Some of them sitting for a better view up on top of parked cars and sheds and other roofs, all of them spreading down the streets and drives and round the cul de sacs, pushing into the waste lots and the fields and the outskirts, lining the roads and the motorway further than the eye, a great greyed carpet studded with lost things, and there was only one thing left for me to do. The silence like a cheer going up, roaring round my head when, flung into the air, diving like a bad swimmer into it, I went over the edge.

For a moment she held me, lightened, delighted. Then she hovered above me like a piece of litter caught up in a crosswind.

For a moment, it's true, I was falling free, suspended by nothing.

Christ but something's really aching somewhere.

God, though, what a beautiful day.

blank card

A bunch of flowers came for me. An old man brought them in his flower shop van. When I opened the front door he said my name like it had a question mark after it.

Yes? I said.

He handed me a bouquet the size of half my body, wrapped up in cellophane.

Thank you, I said.

Pleasure's all mine, he said. I have the best job in the world, delivering flowers to ladies every day of the week except Sundays. Course, sometimes it's funerals and hospitals, but not this one my darling.

I thanked him again, shut the door and took the flowers through to the kitchen. I thought how very lovely and charming it was of you to send them. There were so many and they looked so expensive that I knew they must have cost you a lot of money. I wondered what I'd done, then I wondered what you'd been doing, to make you want to send them. Warning, the label said. Pollen may stain. I sliced through the cellophane sheath with the kitchen knife and took them out. There were sixteen long-stemmed pink roses and a lot of ferny stuff. There were pink and white carnations, and twelve red-tinged big-tongued lilies. There were purple freesias and a lot of little flowering things, and several other types of flower I have never known the names of. I got out all of our vases, filled them with water and divided the powder in the flower-food sachet between them. There still weren't enough vases for all the flowers.

I heard your key in the front door.

They're so beautiful, I called through.

Who is? you said. Me?

No, the flowers, I said.

You don't think I'm beautiful? you called from the hall. When did you stop thinking I'm beautiful? This is terrible. The end of my world.

The flowers, I said again. They just came half an hour ago. Look at them. You're so romantic.

What? you said coming through. Where did you get all these flowers? They must have cost a fortune. No, you said smiling, I didn't send them. You shook your head, laughing. You stopped laughing. I didn't send flowers, you said. They're not from me. You weren't smiling. You shook your head. I didn't send you these flowers, you said.

I dug the envelope out from in among the rubbish. It was wet from the cut stems, stuck with tape on to the cellophane under the ferns I'd thrown away. I peeled it open. There was a card inside. I took it out and turned it over.

Except for the printed illustration of a flower, it was blank.

I turned the empty envelope inside out and I showed you the card. We stared at the crowd of flowers lying piled on the chopping board waiting to be cut, and standing arranged in their vases hanging their eyeless open-mouthed heads. Already they were beginning to smell. The kitchen was full of the collision of their different scents.

You must know who they're from, you said again later. You must have some idea.

I haven't, I said again. I haven't any idea. Honest. I can't think of a single person they could be from. They could be from anybody. There's nobody they could be from. I don't know who they're from.

I said this several times. You said several times how I must have some idea, and each time we said something, whatever I said sounded more like a lie and whatever you said sounded more incredulous. The flowers were still there, in the kitchen. The card and the torn envelope were on the mantelpiece in the front room, evidence, though neither of us could say what of.

Right, you said, and stood up. I'm going to get ready. We can't be late again. It's just not funny. We were late the last time.

That evening we were supposed to be going out to dinner with some friends who were passing through town, and the age-old joke about us was – is – that we're always late, even for dinners we make for friends at our own house. While you were in the shower I propped open the lid of the bin in the kitchen, loaded as many of the flowers as I could into my arms and pushed and snapped their heads and stems down into it. I scraped the waiting flowers off the chopping board in after them and picked all the stray bits of stem and fern and minute flower faces off the table and threw them in too. I had to pile all of the old newspapers for recycling on to the bin to keep it shut. By the time I heard you switch off the shower I had emptied and rinsed the vases and tidied them away, and by the time you came back into the kitchen the table was cleared and all that was left of the flowers was the fact that they'd gone.

You rubbed your head with the towel. Water rolled down your face and neck. You looked at me, straight at me. With your hair wet all over your head like that, you looked crushed.

We can be late one more time, I said, taking your wet hand and leading you back into the bathroom, in behind the shower curtain.

Later, when we were seriously late again, and I was alone in my room drying myself in front of the mirror, hurrying because you were pacing back and fore, looking at your watch, dressed and ready in front of the off television downstairs, I realized that with the big light on in the bedroom and the window blind still up anybody could be watching me out there in the dark.

I stopped what I was doing. Anybody could be standing out there able to see me, nearly naked. Maybe the person who had sent me the flowers could see me, nearly naked.

I shrugged the towel off my shoulders, let my arms relax so that both the towels fell on to the bed and the floor. I watched myself in the mirror and it was as if there were a larger mirror all round me, or as if I were watching a film showing me every move I made, every touch and adjustment I gave to myself. I brushed my hair and it was as if I could see myself from outside myself, brushing my hair.

Close up to the mirror I saw me, shining and excited, naked and full of potential, reflected in the tiny liquid surfaces of my own eyes.

I haven't had so much sex in months, you said after we got home, both of us stretched out on each other on the couch after I'd made intent love to you again in a brilliant performance. Twice in one day, you said, it's just like the old days. I'll have to be the person who hasn't sent you flowers more often.

I stroked your hair, smelled you on my hand, and I thought of how it looked, how it would look to someone who was watching, to be stroking your hair and having this secret moment of recognition.

You were talking. Do you think, you were saying, they might be from someone at your work? Could they be from a client, or a company? like a bribe? Do you think they're maybe from your mother, or your sister, and the card maybe didn't get written on by mistake? It could happen, couldn't it? Have you done anything especially nice for anyone, any of the neighbours, any friends or anything? Anyone that comes to mind? Or is it maybe, is it any kind of anniversary you had with someone before me? one of your old lovers?

Over supper I had thought through various options like these myself, and had decided, while we were all chatting amiably over the dessert menu, that it was much more romantic and exciting if I didn't know whom they were from.

Don't know, I said, as I slipped my hand down inside your opened jeans, watching myself slipping my hand down inside your opened jeans.

What? again? Not again, you said, groaning with pleasure and effort, turning in towards me.

You slept well that night. I lay beside you and heard your regular breathing, deep and sound. I couldn't get to sleep for a long time, partly because I was too pleased with myself, and partly because somewhere at the back of this I was beginning to feel a little edgy. What if someone really was outside, watching our house? I sat up, hugged my knees. What if someone really was there, out there, wondering if I was asleep or not, and what if it was a mad person, whom I knew, or only knew slightly, or didn't know at all; someone who'd seen me at the bus stop or on the street or through the window at my work and had decided that seeing me was enough, that now he or she had some right to me because of it?

I got up and went to the window. I peered out past

the edge of the blind, not moving it in case anybody saw. I stood there for half an hour, then I came back to bed, but I couldn't sleep for seeing myself lying in bed, unable to sleep. Eventually I dozed, woke at first light with birds singing through my dream, my mouth full of flowers, curlicued fronds and the sodden bad-smelling ends of stems; flowers and greenage spewing and trailing up my throat and out of my mouth, ears, nose, all over the floor. After that I slept, and in the morning as soon as I opened my eyes the taste in my mouth was medicinal. Worse than that; there I was, watching myself open my eyes.

I washed my face. I cleaned my teeth. I walked down the hall and down the stairs. I opened the coffee jar, spooned coffee into a cup and pressed the switch on the back of the kettle. I spilled coffee on the table. I wiped it up. I closed my eyes as I wiped, so I wouldn't see myself doing it.

You had gone to work already and had left me a note, folded by the phone on the hallstand. I closed the curtains in the kitchen in case the mad person could see, and sat in the blocked light reading your note. I read it with my hand curled round it, holding it close to my face, until I realised I was shielding it like a child would shield work at school from others who might try to copy it.

Your note was very romantic. In fact it was the most urgent and passionate note you had left me for a long time, possibly as long as several years, several summers; I couldn't remember when the last time was that we'd prowled around our house, alert and waiting, leaving each other notes like this one. *Imagine me round you, at you all day,* the note said at the end, *gently pushing and grazing at you like a cat wiping the scent from its soft black mouth on to the budded tips of the branches of a tree whose roots are covered with its own fallen blossom, surrounded in a ring of sheer petalled whiteness.* It moved me terribly. I began thinking up similar urgent and moving things I could say to you if I telephoned you at work; things so private that when I said them low, down the receiver into your ear, the space between you and whatever you were working on, and you and the other voices I could always hear round you, all those other people who were always in the room with you, would zone and thicken away into a perfect glassy distance.

I looked at the clock. You wouldn't even have got to work yet. I'd have to wait about half an hour to say any of the things. I made the rest of my breakfast behind the closed curtains, thinking of more and more outrageous and daring things to say to you.

But when I opened the lid of the bin to throw away the squeezed orange halves, the bin was full of the flowers. They were still alive, but they were visibly dying. A smell came off them, sweet and rich.

I fetched the blank card and the envelope off the mantelpiece and put them down in front of me on the kitchen table. I stared hard at the only thing on the card, the illustration of the flower – a small yellow one, like a cowslip or primrose – until it looked back out at me so blindly and manufacturedly that something about it made me completely irrelevant.

Bolshy, I called up the shop whose address and telephone number were on the envelope.

Oh I'm sorry madam, the girl said. We can't give out that kind of confidential information, because of its confidentiality.

I asked to speak to the manager.

I'm so sorry, the manager said. I'd like to be able to help you. But it's against our policy to.

I put the phone down. I thought about calling back and pretending to be a police officer or someone in a credit card fraud office. Instead, I called your work number. You answered.

Yes? you said, and although my head had been full of all the sweet, obscene and pretty things I had planned to say to you, I found myself saying nothing at all.

Hello? you said. You said your name, then you said again, hello? Hello?

I was barely able to control my own breathing. It bulletted about high in my chest, as if I'd been running, or as if we'd been hiding from each other and now here I was, well back in the doorway of one of the upstairs rooms, waiting to jump out on you, and you creeping closer along the stealthy hall.

Hello? you said for the final time, sounding angry. Listen, I'm going to hang up, you said. Then you said, oh. Is it you? It's you, isn't it?

I held my breath. Phone air buzzed in my ear.

Hello you, you said. I was hoping you'd call. I

know it's you. I know you're there. I can hear you. Listen.

You began to whisper down the phone, and with all the office noises behind you, someone whistling, someone else yelling across the room, with the high thinned-out voices of other women and men echoing behind it, into my silence you poured a sensualism so potent, so unexpected and so very like you that it made me cough, laugh out loud, and I had to cover the receiver and hang up so you wouldn't hear me choking on my own delight.

It was only after I hung up that I wondered if the you you believed you were talking to on the phone was definitely me after all.

I went back into the kitchen. I got one of the roses out of the rubbish. Its head, still quite tightly closed, was loose and heavy on the end of its drying stem. I propped it up with my finger and then I let it fall again; I ran the tip of my finger over its petals all tucked in on themselves. I held the rose to my nose. It smelt of sweating greenhouses, of all the stuff that you and I routinely throw out, and at the back of this it smelt a little like a rose.

I watched how the rose whorled into itself. I thought of what it was like to be made love to by you, how I knew every inch of it and was still caught out by it, the surprise of your hand on me and your mouth down and over my stomach. My stomach contracted, my insides jumped, unseen, as if touched.

I opened the curtains. I opened the back door and

the spring air came in, smelling of leaves. I opened the cupboard, took out one of the vases, ran some water into it. I put the rose in, took it out again and cut the end off its stem and put it back in the water. Now the vase was too big for the rose; it rested its head on the rim.

With one hand I screwed up the blank card and threw it away. With the other I fished out as many of the flowers as I could, all the ones that had survived the night without water, and all the ones that looked like they would revive given half a chance.

I washed my hands and called the flower shop back. I acted like a new person. I don't think the girl recognized me.

I'd like to send some flowers, I said.

I told them your work address, and gave them my credit card number.

Just leave it blank, I said. She'll know who they're from.

more than one story

It is a Wednesday, half day, early afternoon just after lunch. The man comes out of his wife's summer-house and sees a young woman, not much more than a girl, sitting high on the flat roof of the extension of the rented house two houses along. She is taking her blouse off. She has nothing else on underneath.

It is June. There is a thin skin of birdsong and a noise of insects, the noise of an aeroplane fading at the back of the sky. The woman sunbathing on the roof puts down the book she is half-heartedly skimming. She unbuttons her shirt, glances over the back garden of the house, overgrown, flyblown, not her responsibility. Below her are the other gardens with their trees and neat shrubs, and the mossed-in smouldery lane where burglars lurk at night between the fences which box the gardens off. She sees a man, a bit older than her father, coming out of a shed and turning and going back into it as if he has forgotten something.

A stupefied bee blunders over her. She picks up her book again.

He is hiding in the summerhouse, standing in the smell of creosote behind walls which he knows will give him trouble in a few months' time with the first real storm of the autumn. He runs his hand over the wood, and though he doesn't register it in so many words, he can feel it, the difference between smooth and splintered.

He has taken his spectacles off. They're in his other hand. He weighs them for a moment, looks at them, and puts them down on the table on the pile of his wife's paperbacks. She won't keep the paperbacks in the house because the creases in the spines after she's read them tend to catch the light wherever they're put in a room. She prefers to keep them out here, in her summerhouse.

He unfolds one of the chairs and sits down. With his spectacles upside down on the books, if he focuses hard through one of the lenses out of the window (in the opposite direction from the girl with no clothes on) the lens magnifies the highest tip of a pine tree in someone's garden several streets away. It is as if this particular tree pointing to the sky has been set apart, stronger, bigger, more special than other trees. But, and here's the thing. If he moves – and it only takes the smallest of movements of the head – so as to direct his gaze through the light in the other lens, an inch away from the first, then all he can see of the tree and the world outside is a smashed mess of detailless green, a blur of fir. Now. This is very interesting. It needs some thinking about.

The story of life is simple. The story of life is this. You put one bulb in a pot and water it, and nothing will grow out of it. Six months later you will still be staring at mud. But you put another in another pot and water it, and up come the leaves, tall, green and stately, and in no time at all there's a lily, and not just any ordinary lily, but one of the exotic kind that saints carry in paintings.

There is a lesson in that. He feels a little better now. He closes his eyes, shifts his weight well back into the chair, and tells this to that girl on the extension roof:

When I was a boy, thirteen years old, and that's only a few years younger than you by the looks of it: when I was a boy my brother was crossing the road and he was hit by a careless motorist and he died. He was only ten, only ten years old. They brought him home with his hood up and a bruise above his right eye, his legs sticking out below his duffel coat. One of his socks was down around his ankle, the other was still up at his knee. They were grey, his socks. They were his school socks.

My father walked up and down on the carpet. My mother sat in her chair with her hands over her mouth. The vicar came round. He shook hands with my father and nodded at me. He sat beside my mother on a kitchen chair and said, Mrs Warner, the tragedies of life are brutally impolite. After he'd gone my father took too much for the first time, at least I assume it was the first, and there were plenty more times to come before the last. When I think of it now, which I rarely do, I rarely do. But when I do, which is rare, like I say, I think maybe that vicar hadn't actually known any real tragedies of life; that the real tragedies of life come at you with the smell and the diction of a drunk man, a man you usually know as sober, who recognizes you and comes at you over a perfectly level pavement as if he is walking on the surface of a rough day at sea. So what do you think of that, eh? What do you think of that?

Now he is speaking out loud. The man sent flowers, he says. He came to the door once, but I didn't see him. His car, though. It was a big car, a 1954 Standard 10. They had an engine grille at the front like an open mouth, and lights like two round eyes, like eyes above a downturned open mouth. They were quite high off the ground compared to cars now, big and square, and a couple of weeks after the funeral I saw one in the town parked outside the post office with the engine running and the door open. I don't think it could have been the one, all the same I went down to the river wall and found a stone and came back up to the road, quick in case I missed it, but it was still there, and when no one was looking I took the edge of the stone and went right along the side of it taking the paint off.

I kept that stone. I took it home. At nights I chipped at it with a knife to give it teeth. Right through my teens I had that stone in my pocket. Saturdays would come and I would get the bus into the city, there was a place where they'd park their cars, and I would go round looking for Standards. One Saturday I got five; they were popular cars, the Standards. There was the Standard Pennant too after the Standard 10s; they were a bit bigger. But I was a purist. I only went for the 10s.

Then they got old-fashioned, the type of car that hit him. The Standard Company went; British Leyland closed them down, 1963. You still see Standards on old films. I don't think I've seen a Standard in the street since I was in my thirties. But I kept the stone in my pocket for a long time. It had flecks of white in it in the grey, and the bits of paint caught in the cracks. I can remember that stone, the feel and the look and the weight of it, a lot more clearly than I can remember my brother.

There was one day when there was a 10, a beauty, outside the pub. First I'd heard it behind me – I knew their engines – and then I watched it pass me, and then I followed it up the road and it stopped outside the pub. They had rooms there, people used to stay over-night, it was an inn. But after he parked it the man inside it didn't get out. He sat in his car and he didn't move. I climbed up on to the pub wall to wait. I was out of breath from running. It was winter and it was getting dark, and I knew if I didn't get home soon there would be more trouble than it was worth, and I didn't want to upset her, my mother, but the stone was turning in my hand and the car right in front of me, waiting.

A girl lived at the pub; she was the publican's daughter. Her name was Olive. She was two or three years older than me, and she was working in the pub kitchen. She must have seen me on their wall because the back door opened and out she came across the yard towards me. I knew who she was. It wasn't a very big town then. She'd have known who I was too. I thought she'd be coming to tell me not to sit on their wall, so I pretended I hadn't seen her, I sat there, I poked and scraped at the moss on the top of the wall with my thumbnail. But she shinned up and sat just along from me.

I wasn't supposed to talk to her. She lived at the pub and we lived near the Grange. It was cold, and she didn't have a coat on, just a woollen kind of jersey thing with the collar turned up. She said, what're you doing out here? It's freezing. You've been here for ages. Are you waiting for someone? You'll get a chill in your kidneys if you sit on this cold stone much longer.

You're sitting on it too, I said.

He talks, she said. A miracle. Then she said, it's warmer in our shed.

I'm not cold, I said. Anyway, I'm busy. I'm busy, go away.

There's no need to be rude, she said.

Well she was right about that. So I went with her to their shed, and she shut the door. Now if you could just close your eyes, she said. Though to tell you the truth it was darker in there than it was outside. And if you could give me your hand, she said.

Which hand? I said. Either one, she said, though if she'd said the right or the left I'd surely have given her the wrong one out of fear or something like it. So I held a hand out in the air and she took it, and warmed it up by rubbing my fingers between her own hands, she did it quite roughly, quite briskly, and when she thought it was warmed enough she slipped it, still in her own hand, somewhere warmer still.

I opened my eyes. My hand was under her jersey. Please keep your eyes closed, she said. Thank you.

I did as she asked. She took her own hand away, leaving mine in there to feel. It was small and full, and warm, the first one, and it surprised me, it changed under my hand, it moved; they both did, between soft and hard, blunt and pointed at the same time.

She drew my hand out and she sent me away. You're warmer now, she said. And then by the time I got to the front of the pub again I'd almost forgotten the Standard, but there it was, empty at last so I scraped the paint off in one long curve all the way from the driver's door to the rear fender and ran for home.

The man is laughing. God bless her, I was freezing. My hand must have been freezing, he says. He shakes his head. His shoulders shake with laughter and he wipes at his eyes. The Anchor, he says to himself. Olive. They were small. It was an act of kindness. It was two. She had small acts of kindness, that girl Olive, from the Anchor.

He turns and looks over his shoulder, towards where he knows the girl is sitting, that girl over there on the roof, who lives in the rented house. The people who live there are usually students; they change every year. Years go by and they're always different and that makes them all the same. His wife looks out of the front window every September and says the same thing. Well, that's the summer away. That's the year gone. The students are back.

They're always noisy. Their garden is always a mess, front and back. Ten years ago now, maybe more, they had a party in that house where some of them were so brash and drunken that they took articles of May Henderson at number 30's underwear off her line and posted it to her through her own letterbox.

He won't be able to see anything with his glasses off. He takes his glasses-case out of his pocket, picks his glasses up off the top of the books, snaps them into the case and puts the case in his pocket. He stands up and hoists the chair right round to face the other way. He adjusts the angle, and when he thinks he's probably got it right, he sits down again.

Now when he stares hard screwing up his eyes at the blur ahead of him, he will know it is a girl with no clothes on.

She is reading a book. She is on page fifty-two and there are over three hundred and fifty pages. The book is fashionable, one of the books you're supposed to be reading, that everybody says everybody should read because it is about now. There are three hundred and seven pages still to go. She was lucky to get on the summer course this book is taught on; it was heavily oversubscribed. There are twenty-three more pages until the end of the chapter. For the last couple of minutes she has been reading a sentence then reading the same sentence over again by mistake. Right now she is stuck on the word *fucking* in the phrase *this fucking shit man*.

She draws a line in the margin beside it and puts the book down. This morning a man came to the door and asked if he could clean the windows in the house. He looked quite old, about thirty, he looked the unemployed sort, and he was carrying a ladder. He said he'd do them for five pounds, and then he knocked on the back door and said, I've cut my knee on my ladder, do you have a plaster, can I come in and clean it up in your bathroom? His knee was bleeding through a rip in his jeans.

He'd come through along the hall from the bath-room with his jeans round his ankles and a skin-coloured Band-Aid in his hand. Would you put it on for me? he said, I can't stand the sight of blood. So she bent down and wiped his knee with a tissue and peeled the plaster open and put it over his cut, which was just a tiny graze under all the blood. Thanks, the man said, and then he swayed himself inside his shorts at her, just by her head. No thanks, she said. Just the windows, okay?

Actually she hadn't said anything, but when she tells it later, she could say that's what she said. No thanks, just the windows today thanks. Actually she'd been a little shocked; it was quite shocking, though it isn't supposed to be. She stood up, left him standing, went back to her room; she saw him in the hall mirror going back to the bathroom holding his jeans up. After that he cleaned the windows and when he was finished she told him, come back at seven tonight so I can collect the money from my flatmates.

It will be a good story to tell. He was quite nice really. He could have been horrible. It'll be funny later.

Something has landed on her breast. It walks across above her nipple then flies off. She slaps too late at the slight itch where it walked. It is so hot today that the tar on the roof is beginning to melt in some places, and the black of it has seeped into the top of her towel above her head. She jerks the towel off the tar, straightens it, and lies back down.

Three years ago is so long ago it seems like three lives ago. The bus lurched round a corner and Sharon Neil put her hand on, took it off, no one saw; sorry she said, the bus lurching like that was her excuse. Nice though, eh? Sharon Neil had said, not looking at her, looking straight ahead.

Sharon Neil, never just Sharon, always Sharon Neil, always her full name; she couldn't think of her without her surname; she didn't know why. Sharon Neil was a year older and worked full time at General Accident, down the corridor in the claims room. She dealt with the things the summer girls weren't qualified to. You're a quiet one, aren't you? always reading; books mean next to nothing to me, can't be arsed with them, all

those words, what're you reading today? she'd said in
the tea room, sitting down next to her. With the top
button of her work blouse undone at her throat,
upstairs on the bus she had touched here, on the breast,
on the left. Her mother had a Lada, and when Sharon
Neil passed her driving test she was allowed to drive it;
she drew up beside her one day, drove the car almost
up the kerb – hey, you, you want a lift home? – and
instead of driving her home drove her four or five miles
out of town, all the way out the old road to the Electric
Hill, where they were building the crematorium.

Sharon Neil stopped the car in the middle of the road
halfway down the hill. She switched the ignition off.
The road was single track but there were no other cars
coming, though you could hear the builders in the near
distance.

Watch this, she said. It's really something.

She took her foot off the brake and the car started to
freewheel backwards. It rolled backwards up the hill by
itself as if something were pulling it.

The woman lies on the roof looking at the blue of
the sky without seeing anything.

The car went two thirds of the way up the hill backwards as if by magic.

How did you do that? she'd said.

I'm not doing anything, Sharon Neil said. It's the
road we're on. It's an invisible force field. I'd have
thought you'd have known that, professor. Either that
or it's a trick of the light. It looks like we're going
downhill but really the slope is going the other way.

Really we weren't driving downhill in the first place because really what looks like it'll be one thing is another.

She was sitting next to Sharon Neil in the passenger seat. Do it again, she said. Sharon started the car up, drove it forward a hundred yards, cut the engine and took her feet off the pedals, let it roll slowly back up.

Do it again. Sharon Neil knew everything without being told anything. After the Electric Hill she drove to a place in the woods up past the golf course, and looking at her watch, then out of the front windscreen at the quiet trees, she said, well do you want to get into the back then, because we haven't much time, she's wanting the car back at six.

That was something. At least that was something, that hour in the car, though Sharon Neil did it like she was running for a bus she was determined not to miss. At least there was something about it, even so, in the back of the car, with the tiny holes punched in the stuff that padded its roof and above its doors, with the windows down and the smell of pine and earth coming through.

She imagines it had been Sharon Neil who'd come to the door this morning asking to clean the windows. Imagine if she'd opened the door and there she was. Or maybe not, maybe that'd be too embarrassing, but maybe someone like her, asking to fill her bucket with soapy water from the kitchen tap, then coming through from the bathroom with her jeans undone. But it's all too cheap. It isn't what she wants.

That must be why it's called Electric Hill, Sharon
Neil said. It's something to do with some kind of elec-
trics; something pulls us backwards even though it
looks like we should be going forwards. Then she
reached over and took her hand, and placed it high up
on her nyloned thigh, and the shock went through her
for the first time as Sharon Neil, grinning, started up
the car again and drove off, forwards; those shocking
muscles under her hand something to do with the speed
and the swerve of the car as they sailed past the fields
dug up for the crematorium foundations, the builders'
trucks and rows of bricks and concrete pipes.

I could teach you to drive if you like before you go to
the university, she said afterwards on the way home.
We've a couple of months. I'm teaching my boyfriend.
But I'd better not see too much of you, had I, or
people'll get suspicious. And later, at the end of the
summer, Sharon Neil had showed the girls at work the
engagement ring her boyfriend Bernard had bought
her, and the girls all round the office squealed and
shrieked about it.

It was pretty good of her really, she tells the gardens,
the fences, the nobody below her; she came up to me at
half-past five when I was putting on my coat to go. We
were usually careful, we usually ignored each other at
work. And she looked at me, right at me, full into my
eyes in front of everyone, and said, now if you ever
want those driving lessons, prof., just give me a call,
I'm getting my own car soon and I'd trust you, I think,
you of all people. You're good behind the wheel.

Me of all people. The sun dips behind the tops of the houses on the street opposite and the light diminishes round her. She pushes herself up on her elbows and sits hugging her knees on the gritty roof. Because it was thoughtful of her, she says to herself. She was a thoughtful person, Sharon Neil. She meant well.

She squints down at herself. Her chest is burned, but not too much; the red goes white almost as soon as she touches it. By tomorrow or the next day it will be a nice even brown.

She sits up properly, closes the book, pulls her shirt on over her head.

The man comes out of the summerhouse putting his glasses on. He glances, quick, off to the side, but it's all right. She's not nude any more.

With her head through the neckhole of her shirt the woman sees the old man coming out of his shed. She scrapes at the hardened tar stuck on her towel.

He comes up through his garden, and she gathers her things together, gets ready to shin down the side of the extension.

Nice old man, she thinks. They like gardening, old men like him.

Eighteen, nineteen, he thinks. Older than I thought. Still, a child. She'll be gone in three weeks.

They smile at each other, the polite way you do when you don't know somebody but you want to be nice.

Hopefully be another sunny one tomorrow, he shouts up.

She can't hear what he's saying, but she nods and smiles. He lifts his hand, tentative. She waves back, shy acknowledgement, yes, hello, goodbye.

small deaths

Halfway through the summer the weather suddenly got better, hotter. For nearly a week the air was hot, hanging in the house as thick as smoke, hanging around the garden curling and deadening the leaves. I love it, you said. I love this weather. I love you.

I sat in your deckchair and read, or watched you. You lay on your front on my turkish rug in the grass and read the paper, and rolled on to your back, smiled up at me from beneath your hand. We took turns in and out of the shade. The cat was asleep under the chair, waking only every so often to scratch lazily behind his head. Your newspaper blew across the garden and yellowed in the heat all afternoon. You were asleep and I was almost asleep when a small striped insect, like a wasp without a sting, landed on my hand and climbed my arm; I could feel the pinpoints of its legs between the hairs; I watched it cross the crease where my arm was bent as if the crease was the finishing line of a race, and launch itself off again, battering into the air with its very small wings.

It was the perfect day today, I said. Yes, you said, I could live in a climate like this. I wish we lived in a climate like this all the time.

Halfway through the week, when the air had become thunderous and the sun had turned into intermittent grey rain, we woke up to them everywhere in the house. They were in the carpets of all the rooms and in the stair carpet and the hall carpet, and they were jumping about on the linoleum in the kitchen over by the sink. They were in the pile of clean clothes by the bedroom door. They were in the bed. I sat up and picked something black off my leg and it jumped out from between my finger and thumb before I had the chance to see what it was. I picked three more off one at a time, holding them very tightly between the tips of my fingers, and one by one I dropped them all out of the bedroom window. I came downstairs. By the time I got to the bottom I had another three on one leg and two on the other foot. I saw the cat skipping and leaping across the back room like a cartoon cat, like a cat walking on nippy coals, trying to keep his paws off the ground.

Even after we used the spray and the sweet-smelling powder, after we'd sprayed and washed and dried all the clothes, sheets and cushion covers, I leaned down to pick up my cup off the floor and there were two, alive, swimming in my tea.

They're good swimmers, you said.

You had been feeding any you found still alive, you told me, to the goldfish, and had been watching how, if the fish didn't see them, they would negotiate the depths, astute as frogmen, until they found a plant in the tank, then they'd climb up it and jump out of the water.

I went through to the bathroom to fetch the spray we'd used all over the house. It says on here, I said holding it up, that this is very poisonous to goldfish. I read out what was written in block capitals on the side of the can. For use only as an insecticide. For indoor use only. Do not apply to clothing or human bedding. 100 ml of product will treat approximately 35 square metres of surface. Do not breathe spray mist. Cover food, food preparing equipment and eating utensils before application. Do not apply to surfaces on which food is stored, prepared or eaten. Extremely dangerous to fish and other aquatic life. Remove or cover fish tanks and bowls before application.

I carried on reading out what it said. Cover water storage tanks before application. When using do not eat, drink or smoke. Do not apply directly to animals. Exclude animals during application. This material and its container must be disposed of in a safe way. The (COSHH) Control Of Substances Hazardous To Health Regulations 1994 may apply to the use of this product at work. Keep off skin. Wash hands after use. Do not handle treated fabrics until dry and air thoroughly before use. Keep away from food, drink and animal feeding stuffs. Until dry, treated surfaces can pose a fire risk. Keep out of reach of children. Avoid contact with eyes. If in eyes flush with plenty of clean water. Get medical attention if irritation persists. If on skin remove contaminated clothing and wash affected areas with soap and water. Keep away from any source of ignition. No smoking. Read all precautions before use.

Oh, right, you said looking at your hands. Did we do all that?

Yes, of course, I said. I rubbed my eye with my finger. Then I put the can on the table and sat down. Then I went through to wash my hands.

Maybe it needs time to kick in, I called through.

What? you said. When I came back, you were looking hard at the carpet, aimlessly scratching at your bites.

You stopped feeding them to the fish. You started putting the live ones we still found in a glass filled with water instead. They can't climb up the sides of a glass, you said, like they can climb up the sides of a cup or bowl.

The next morning you woke me to show me. Of five that you'd put in a glass the night before, nearly twelve hours ago, three were still swimming on the water, their legs flailing against the side of the glass and sending currents we couldn't see across the surface. You held the glass up so I could look through the base. One was lying drowned at the bottom. The glass magnified it. Its legs were minuscule eyelash hairs and its body the slightest paring of a nail.

You were excited. See? you said. There's one missing. I put five in, there's only four. One's got out.

We decided that the missing one could only have escaped by getting up on to the back of another and springing out. They can jump as high as six feet, you know, you said, swilling the glass round, trying to sink the three that were left.

When you'd gone to work, I took the glass with them still swimming in it outside, out of the house and out of the garden, and poured the contents into the weeds on the traffic island at the corner. I put the glass in the sink, put half an inch of washing up liquid into the bottom of it, filled the rest up with water and left it to soak.

All day I felt them jumping against my legs but every time I stopped to look there was nothing there. I put down my pen and listened to nothing. Down there between the rucks of dust, deep in the shoddy globules of carpet, the choking corpses, the choked hatchings of their eggs.

But that evening, while we were watching an old horror film on television, I picked one, black and juicy and healthy, off the inside of my upper lip.

Oh, Jesus, I said.

Right, you said. Right. That's it.

We took the cat to the vet's. The vet gave us an even stronger insecticide. There's been an epidemic, he said. I'm nearly out of this. The whole of town has broken out. He showed us the dust and dirt and insect leavings inside the cat's fur and gave us three small plastic containers full of insecticide, which he told us to apply to the skin at the back of the cat's neck and between his shoulders. He felt all over the cat's body, checking his kidneys and liver and stomach, and looked in the cat's eyes, and took the cat's temperature.

I think we'll hang on to him overnight, he said. His temperature's very high. There's a couple of tests I'd like to run, if that's all right with you.

We made an arrangement with the receptionist to pay when we knew the whole cost, and we took turns carrying the empty cat box across the park. People with children who went past us in the park tried to see inside the box, in case there was something cute.

When we got home we went from room to room upstairs and down, evenly spraying the floors and the furnishings with the new canisters and shutting each door behind us. Finally you sprayed the hall and the stair carpet and ran for the front door holding your breath. We sat on the wall outside. We had to sit outside for half an hour at least; it said on the can that rooms shouldn't be aired for at least half an hour and if possible should be left overnight. The insecticide, however, if applied properly, would last seven months.

One of the neighbours across the road waved to us from her front window. We waved back.

Luckily for us out there on the wall, the rain of the past few days had stopped. Luckily, it was quite a dry evening.

You looked at your watch. Twenty-six minutes to go, you said.

We sat in the low evening sun and waited for the twenty-six minutes to pass.

virtual

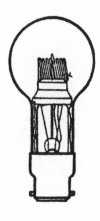

The girl in the bed opposite was very beautiful. She had dark hair and dark eyes and the paleness and seriousness of face of one of those painted Pre-Raphaelite heroines, and it was only when the nurse came in and the girl peeled back the blankets she'd coiled round and over her, and slowly pushed herself up off the bed, that she was shocking. The nurse helped her balance on the metal scaffold and inch her way across from the bed to the bathroom at the end of the ward. Her arms were like the arms of a starving child. Her legs, swollen by the huge knuckles of their knees and ankles, were like the legs of one of those white bodies from the last war dead on the ground and bull-dozed into a pit; they moved beneath the zimmer like something practical and ghastly was making them move.

What's wrong with her? I asked my aunt in a whisper.

I thought to myself that it must be something terrible. She looked thin enough to be dead or dying.

She's a poor thing, my aunt said. She's an awful nice girl. She's awful clever. She does the crosswords for us, she knows all the words. She was at the university but she had to stop.

Then she leaned forward and whispered to me. There's nothing actually wrong with her so to speak. She just won't eat.

My aunt was in hospital for what she called something unmentionable down there. Something unmentionable down there had worn out, she told me when we met on the street a few days ago, and she had to come in and have it seen to. She's not really my aunt; she is my mother's old friend, one of those friends that get called an aunt; and now she is much older than my mother was when she died, her face much the same, a little more lined and bagged, smiling, ten years on and still thriving. I often wonder how it is that she can still be alive if my mother is dead, how it can be that my mother is dead if her friend is still so alive. It doesn't seem possible that one person can just be gone like that and another can still be here, shopping in the same shops or walking along the same pavements or drinking tea out of some of the very same cups even, but it is, it's the most possible, most everyday thing in the world.

It was good of you to come in and see me, she said, her hand on my arm, her too familiar face close to mine. And the flowers are lovely. She gave me a dry

kiss on the cheek. The old skin folded along the
hollows of her throat and stretched at her collarbone.
She smelt of her house and she smelt of something else,
the ward maybe, and she waved me goodbye as I left.
I waved back.

I passed the thin girl on my way out; she was
hunched in blankets, a blanket over her legs, a blanket
piled over her stomach. She smiled a polite goodbye at
me too. Goodbye. I smiled back.

But that night, as I ate supper, I stuck the fork in the
food and rolled it on to the prongs, I held it in front of
my mouth, then I put it inside my mouth and closed my
lips and pulled the fork out, felt the food on my tongue,
chewed and swallowed the food. I thought about the
thin girl. I wondered what her name was. I wondered if
there was anything she wanted, anything she would
like.

I went back to the hospital the next day.

What a surprise! my aunt said. But you'd no need to
come again. I told you yesterday. I'm just about better.

She was sitting up in a chair, wearing her clothes.

Oh, you know, I said. I was passing, I thought you
could do with a visitor. And I was wondering if there
was anything I could bring you, anything I could do for
you, shopping, anything?

But you know I'll be out tomorrow, my aunt said.
She shook her newspaper and folded it down,
smoothed it out on the bed, shook her head for the
benefit of the new lady in the bed next to her. First I
don't see her for years, eh Edith, she said, then I can't

get rid of her. Doesn't she have a job to go to? She turned to me. What am I going to do with you? What would your mother say to that, eh? her bad daughter being so good at last?

She told me again the details of her operation, all the time really telling them to Edith who was listening and nodding and adding her own commentary. I sneaked a look across. She was still there, she was asleep. She looked like a broken child.

Actually, my aunt was saying, there is something. If you've the time, only if you've the time, mind. You couldn't nip into the house and feed the fish for me. I'm worried one more day might be just one day too many. I'm not wanting them to start eating each other. Here's the key. You only need the one key. Leave it in the geranium on the left-hand side of the mat on your way out.

Her fish were the small kind, the white ones, I don't know the name of the type. They eat flakes of food out of a plastic container. The flakes have been made out of vegetable matter and bits of different species of fish. You're only supposed to give them a pinch of it, they're supposed to need very little. They swarmed together to the surface to be fed and I poured it out on to their heads, I poured far too much by mistake so that they were swimming in a riot of food spread across the surface of the water, red and yellow and gold. The fish lashed and fought in the food. The smallest ones, too small to fight, waited lower down in the tank for the crumbs of flake to sink to their level.

I had remembered the way to her house. I could have found it with my eyes shut, and her house was the same as I remembered. The living room was the same though the tv looked new beside the rest of the furniture; the old one must have given out. I sat on the couch and watched the fish eat. Her house was small, like ours was when I was a child, the same kind of house. My aunt must have bought hers because she'd changed the front door and changed the windows. Apart from these things it was the same, the same as it had been when we came round here and my mother swung me down in front of the television, she and my aunt in the kitchen doing some serious talking in low voices under the smell and the slow veil of cigarette smoke, the hushed tone of agreement between them, the occasional conspiratorial hushed whoop of a laugh. Can a laugh be hushed and a whoop at the same time? Theirs was, their laughter, it was both; raucous and subdued, wild and withheld; it somehow wouldn't have been quite proper otherwise.

Anyway I don't know why I keep calling her my aunt. Habit I suppose. Because she was just a friend, a friend of the family, my mother had several such friends. I fed the fish for her and I sat on her couch and I wondered what she could have meant, saying I was my mother's bad daughter. My mother's bad daughter. I couldn't think which of the things about me it was, which of the things I might have done, and she might have heard about from someone else in that same hushed secret women's tone, that constituted bad.

Maybe I was about to be bad again, because I couldn't remember which geranium I was supposed to hide the key in. I was sure to get it wrong. I almost wanted to get it wrong on purpose. Maybe that was the kind of thing she meant by bad. Like how I wanted to give the fish even more food than they'd already had, though I knew it wouldn't be good for them. They still looked hungry. They were still acting hungry because they knew the light was on and I hadn't gone yet, I was still somewhere in the room.

I was hungry too, even though I'd eaten all day. All afternoon and all that evening I had been eating things. It's not that I ate more than I usually did, and it's not that I eat any more than the average person. It's just that today, for once, I had simply noticed the casual stream and variety of the things I put in my mouth. I had eaten an apple and a nectarine and some bread and coleslaw for lunch. I had chewed my fingers and the ends of several pens. I had eaten a chocolate bar and what was left of a packet of crisps and the whole of a packet of Polos. I ate a dinner of aubergine, mozzarella, tomato, garlic and pasta all mixed together, and after it I ate some lettuce and another apple. I pulled the string off a herbal tea-bag, prised the little hinge out of the label, put both the label and the string into my mouth and chewed them into little pieces and swallowed them. Then I drove round to feed the fish and on the way I was thinking about what I could buy to eat at the all-night garage on the way back if I stopped for petrol. They do hot snacks there, hot chicken in greaseproof paper, and barbecued ribs and sausages, as well as a range of sweets and more substantial things in tins like ravioli, beans and ambrosia creamed rice.

I fed the fish more fish food. I thought of the thin girl. I thought how maybe I could drive a car full of delicious things from the garage to the hospital and spread them prettily out on the bed to tempt her, so that she would want to eat, so that she wouldn't be able not to eat. But probably there wasn't the kind of thing available at the garage that she'd want to eat. I couldn't think of anything delicious enough, or anything delicate enough for her. I thought harder. Tiny dainty scented seafood. Thin slivers of choicest chicken. Things which I had no idea how to get. But if I could get them, say I could get them, I could spread them out and let her choose. I wondered if she was fasting, like the men in Northern Ireland or the suffragettes, or like saints used to do; I wondered if it was pictures of thin women in magazines that had made her decide she didn't want to eat any more. I wondered what had happened to her. I wondered what would happen if someone picked her up and put their arms around her and hugged her close. She looked thin enough to snap into pieces.

All the way home in the car I thought about what it would be like to have someone snap into pieces in your arms. I couldn't get it out of my head; it made me wince, it made my stomach wince to think about it, but I thought about it again and again. The small crack of the bones inside the skin at the slightest pressure, like the snap of dry twigs, or the crack of the shell of a snail under your foot on the pavement before you realize what it is you've done.

Look who's here, my aunt said the next day. Look who's back. I was hoping you'd come. You can give me a lift home.

Her bags were on the bed and the bed was made. I leaned down so she could speak by my ear, but she didn't say anything. She was hiding her hand so only I could see it and jerking her thumb at the old woman next to her, Edith, who looked sweaty and yellow and uncomfortable and was staring into space. My aunt looked at me, shook her head with a slight shake that only I was meant to notice.

Right then, my aunt said cheerily. I'll get myself together.

She moved me out of the way and put her arm in her locker drawer, feeling around to see if she'd missed anything.

A family had gathered round the thin girl opposite. A man sat on the edge of the bed, looked lost and dazed. A small grey woman held one of the girl's hands, telling her things. The girl nodded back, her face white. A small boy, her brother, hung his legs off the chair kicking the metal legs of the zimmer with a dull clanging, and a teenage girl, an inflated version of the pale girl in the bed, poured water from a jug into the plants on the locker table.

I followed my aunt, who had disappeared ahead of

me already, out of the ward. Goodbye, the girl said as I passed.

All the people round her bed turned to look at me, all at once. Her father made room for her to see me, and she shifted up the bed, pained and graceful, and took a moment to find her breath. There was a tube attached to one side of her nose, and to a machine behind the bed.

The girl held her hand up until she was able to speak. Please say goodbye to your mother for me, she said. I didn't get the chance.

Yes, I said.

She couldn't wait to get out of here, the girl said. Me neither. She looks a lot better though, doesn't she?

Yes, I said, she does, doesn't she?

You'll be pleased, the girl said. She smiled. Her lips drew back round very white teeth. The smile made her look tired. She held up something red in her hand, like a plastic keyring. Look what they've brought me today, she said.

I smiled and nodded. It looked like a keyring. I didn't know what it was.

It's a virtual pet, she said.

They're Japanese. She can't have a cat in a hospital and she was missing the cat, her mother said, smiling at me.

Her mother looked tired too. I smiled back.

Look, the girl said. Look what things you can do with it.

The small boy moved his legs like he was told so that

I could come in closer. I put down the case and the bags. The girl showed me how the pet needed baths and games, it needed to be disciplined and taught, and fed and watered, it needed you to push buttons to make sure of all of this, and that it was happy with the amount of heat and light you gave it.

It has this life cycle and you have to get it right, the girl said. Or it dies. It gets a halo above its head and a tombstone. Then she laughed. I hate it, she laughed. It isn't even alive and it's making me feel guilty. Here.

She put the plastic thing in my hand. I turned it over. On a small screen a creature with eyes and no mouth was moving up and down and back and fore very fast in the small space.

The Japanese are fighting over getting these, the father said.

They're really popular, the sister said from behind the bed.

Japanese gangsters are taking over selling them, they're so popular. They're a real fad, the father said.

See, the girl said. It's really irritating.

A noise was coming out of the plastic. The creature was flashing black and white. The girl took it back and peered hard at it. That means it needs a bath, she said. She pressed a series of buttons making a series of beeps. Then she showed me the happy-faced clean creature. It made a melodious beeping sound to show that it was happy.

See? the girl said. It never shuts up.

Everybody laughed. The small boy snorted on the

chair. Well if you want it to shut up you could just take the battery out, he said.

Everybody laughed again.

What? the boy said. Well what? What's so funny? All you need is one of those small screwdrivers. You could just take it out. If it was annoying you so much.

As I went down the corridor my face was sore from all the smiling. I found my aunt and drove her home. I came in with her and made sure her cupboard and her fridge had enough in them to see her through the next few days. Then I drove home. At home I went from room to room in my big house, with all the books and things and furniture and pictures. I looked out of the window at the view over the bridge and the houses. I looked out of the back room at the view over the other back gardens. There was a cat asleep on top of one of the sheds. I thought about getting a cat. Then I thought about maybe getting some fish and a tank.

Up so close to the thin beautiful girl I had seen that the skin round her eyes, the skin that made her eyelids, was loosened and roomy. Her hand up close had been like the foot of a bird and you could see lines in it, and lines along her fingers, like the traceries in a leaf.

I couldn't think what to do.

I couldn't imagine what to do next, or how to be able to do it right.

okay so far

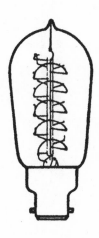

We have come a long way. We have travelled half the world in less than half a day. We've watched films above the Atlantic, we've seen motorways from the tinted windows of Greyhound buses and we've gone back and fore in trams and taxis to and from and round the streets of several cities new to us. This is our first rail journey here, and we are so sophisticated now in our travelling that the inside of the train is far more interesting to us than what's beyond the window.

Inside the train the seats are covered in green leather. They have headrests that are just too high for either of us. Each double set of seats has its own disposable litter bag hung on a small bolt below the window. There are different rules about where you sit and how you get on the train; an escalator took us from the neat queue in the station to the correct platform a few people at a time, and each carriage has its own specifically designated destination. And now here we are, in the right carriage sitting in the right seats.

We have been on this train for four hours. You are still reading the newspaper you bought in the city we left, reading about which films are showing in which cinemas and telling me what we could have gone to see if we had stayed on there. I am watching light from the woods with their shaded patches of pockmarked snow, or light from the winter-empty small towns decrepit with backlots, as it smashes and changes and slides on the green leather headrest in front of me.

A small girl stands up further along the carriage. She looks about nine and she is pushing her arms into the sleeves of a jacket. The man she's been sitting beside, the man I thought was probably her father, doesn't look up. She looks far too young to be travelling by herself. But she is, and she comes down the aisle with her jacket shrugged on over her worn sweatshirt, rumpled, like a child who's just woken up and come to the breakfast table. As she passes our seats she looks straight at us, at me, looks straight at my face, my hair and my clothes. The train slows to a halt and she goes past with the other people waiting to get off.

The train begins to move again. Was that girl travelling by herself? I say.

Looked like it, you say. I think she liked your boots. She was watching us over the back of her seat. Didn't you see her?

No, I say. I didn't even notice her.

You settle back behind your newspaper. She watched us for quite a long time, you say.

I look at my boots, then I stretch my legs out under the seat in front and settle down to doze. Last night we stayed in a Comfort Hotel. There are Comfort Hotels everywhere and we can only just afford them; tonight when we arrive we will be staying in a French version, a Château Comfort. Last night you pulled the covers back, you turned the pillow over so we couldn't see the cigarette burn in the pillowslip, and we lay gingerly apart on the narrow strip of bed avoiding the faded stains and bloodspots left by all the other people. You were lying with your back to me, and in the half-dark lit by the street outside we listened to the rain on the window and the television noise coming through the walls, and we fell to playing one of your games, the one where I have to guess about who's dead and who's still alive.

Kenneth Williams, you said.

Oh, I know this one, I said. He's dead, he's definitely dead.

Right, you said. André Previn.

He's still alive, I said, at least I think he is. Isn't he?

Which, come on, which one is it? you said. He has to be either alive or dead, a pound if you get it wrong.

He's alive, I said.

Right. Arthur Askey.

Dead.

Saul Bellow.

Alive.

Katharine Hepburn.

Alive. Just.

Um . . . Frida Kahlo.

Dead.

Nena.

Who? I said.

Nena. Nena who sang Ninety Nine Red Balloons.

Oh God, I said, I don't know. She's in purgatory.
No, she gets a special medal, a special place in heaven
reserved for people who completely disappear after
they've given themselves over like that.

What do you mean, given themselves over? You
mean she's dead?

No, I mean gave herself over, I said, made up the,
the, you know, backdrop to times of our lives.

The backdrop?

Yeah, you know. The cultural backdrop.

Oh, the *cultural* backdrop. So. She's dead, then? you
said.

No, I was just –

Dead or alive? you said.

Christ, I don't know. Alive.

Hah. Lucky guess, you said.

Anyway, how do *you* know for sure she's alive? I
said. How do you know she's not dead? Maybe she
died earlier this evening. Maybe she's right this minute,
how do you know –

I know everything, you said. Now. Ginger Rogers.

Alive, I said, and you turned with your face so close
to mine that I couldn't see you properly, you were so

close; you made a triumphant noise, two dollars, you said, that's two dollars, altogether that's twenty-eight you owe me, that's fourteen quid. I looked right into your eyes, we were laughing, and I said, Ginger Rogers will never die, she lives forever, she's an immortal and I'm paying you nothing, and we were both laughing, and I open my eyes on the train with you next to me, your newspaper folded on your lap, because I hear you saying something, you say it again for me, where do you think she was going by herself? and I say, who? That girl, you say, the one who was looking at us, the one who got off at the airport stop.

Was it an airport stop? I say. Then she was probably going to the airport.

Yes, you say. Brilliant. But why? Why was she going to the airport? Was she meeting her mother? Was she meeting her father? Where was she flying to? Was she scared of flying?

She didn't look scared, I say, and I think to myself how that small girl, though I only saw her for a few moments, looked like she wouldn't be scared of anything. I think about when I was that age and wasn't scared of anything. I try to remember her looking at us, seeing us so easily together, I picture what you and I must look like together, then I think of her looking at complete strangers with that blank nine-year-old directness. It takes me by surprise that I'm a stranger with clothes and boots on that can be looked at and decided about.

I decide someone was picking her up from outside

the station, waiting in a car to take her home. Then I remember something I haven't thought about for years, my father in the car we had when cars were still like metal shells, and instead of going straight home we drove round by the football field so he could see if there was a game on, and I was leaning against the door and the door swung open, and he reached over from the driver's seat and wrenched me back in by the arm, the car swerving towards the kerb as he caught the door by the window winder and slammed it as shut as it would go, though light and air still came in the crack where the door didn't fit.

Maybe her father, I say, was coming to pick her up at the airport.

No, you say, I think her mother. Her hair needed combed.

Right, I said. So she's obviously been staying with her father and now she's coming home to her mother after a weekend of unwashed clothes and uncombed hair. She stays with her father every third weekend. He lives in Toronto and her mother lives in Montreal. Well, near Montreal, near the airport.

Okay so far, you say. Keep going.

They split up, I say leaning as far back in my seat as the headrest will allow, probably because of the French–English split.

And she goes to her father's house every third weekend, you say, and he takes her to that diner we went to behind that burnt-out cinema and they have the same thing to eat every Sunday.

Burgers, home fries, onion rings and ice-cream, I say since that's what we had when we went there.

Well I don't know, you say. I'm not so sure. She didn't look miserable enough to me, to have parents in two different cities.

Yet another place is veering towards us, its lights in the seeable distance, and you are already flicking through its guide book. I shut my eyes. God help us, my father says. Sit away from the door. So I huddle towards the gearstick, I can't remember the make of the car, I think it was green. God help us, eh? he said again, and nudged me with his elbow. And for God's sake, he said when we drew up outside the house, not a word to your mother, we won't tell her, don't tell, eh?

I didn't tell anyone, not for years, not till I tell you, tonight, in our next hotel. In my memory I am not telling, I'm sitting on the kerb by the car, racing bits of stick across the sky in the puddles and looking at the road, which has the same kind of surface as the one I nearly hit, the one sliding beneath the car an inch from my eye as I hang upside down over it. Some roads have smoothed tarmac that melts in the sun in the summer, it comes off on your feet. My other road, the road I now think of as mine, the road I so nearly grazed, has the kind of surface that could take the skin right off a face.

This latest hotel is a bit old-fashioned, flouncy, a bit flowery, but comfortable, not too worn. We have a back room which means we won't be kept awake by the noise of the traffic. We have spent the evening deciding which things to go and see tomorrow on our one day here, and now you are lying on the bed surrounded by discarded books and half-unfolded maps. It is very warm in the room; the air conditioner is blasting out hot air and we can't get the window to open. You have almost no clothes on; your clothes are in a pile on the floor. The words rise to my mouth, right to the tip of my tongue, how very lovely you are, lying like that, but I sit on the bed and tell you an anecdote instead, about how when I was small I nearly fell out of the car and my father leaned over and caught me just in time.

I had bruising round my wrist from where he caught me, I say, you could see his fingermarks. It took a fortnight to fade and all the boys at school wanted to know how I got it. I told the teacher my wrist was sprained, I told her what my father told my mother, that I'd fallen out of a tree on to it. The teacher let me off sewing and knitting for weeks.

You don't say anything; your eyes are closed. I suppose you're asleep and you haven't heard me. I lie back on my side of the bed. I look at the cornices on the ceiling. This house used to be someone's home. This used to be someone's room, and this is the strangest thing about travelling, that when we get back these rooms and these cities will mean more to us than they do while we're actually here in them; the carrier-bags with the names of museums, art galleries, shops on them will mean more than this does, this lying in a room in just another place breathing its warmed-up air.

I put the light out, and it takes me a while to realize

that you're not asleep at all, that the slight noise I can hear above the air conditioner is you, controlling your breathing so that you won't be heard, holding yourself still so I won't feel any movement of the bed. Later, after you've stopped crying, and when you're in my arms for the first time in a long time, you tell me this story:

Before, every year in the trades fortnight we would go down the east coast, to Filey or Scarborough, Whitby and Whitley Bay, places they could take the caravan. It was just me by then on holiday, eventually there was just me left to take, my sisters all got too old to want to come, and that's how I try to think of it, the three of us all still together, my mother, my father and I in a kind of companionable nothingness, where nobody spoke much, nobody said anything; my mother smoking, her arm out of the open window and her cigarette air blowing into the back of the car where I was sitting with my legs stuck to the car seat in the heat listening to Tony Blackburn on the radio, that song about beach baby beach baby give me your hand, or Gilbert O'Sullivan, that song he had about how good his children were, do you remember? you could tell something sad had happened to the people in the song but the song never told you what, and my father driving with his shirt sleeves rolled up and his shirt undone, and the caravan lurching along behind the car. And then there was always the time when we'd get to the caravan site and my father would put up the awning, he'd be in a foul mood, my mother warning me, leave him, he's putting the awning up. There was this one year, we were in Scarborough, and my parents met this couple, you always met people on caravan sites, and their daughter had died of something, cancer I think, she had really loved riding horses and even though she'd been in this, you know, great pain, she'd still insisted on going out for a ride on a pony, they didn't tell me about any of this, I heard them talk about it days afterwards. That summer the weather was like you imagine when you imagine good weather. I had a kite, it was shaped like an eagle, I ran about so much I got brown all over, people kept thinking I was a boy and I didn't mind, I liked it, I was eleven, not old enough to mind, still young enough to be pleased about it, and anyway all the boys on the site wanted to be my friend because of my kite. That day I came back to the caravan and my parents had met the people whose girl had died, they were all sitting together on those folding seats and talking. My parents had been waiting for me to come back; we were going to a beach. They all looked at me, and then my parents said goodbye to the people, and when I was getting into the car my mother gave me this big hug, when we got to the beach she and my father insisted on buying me a bucket and spade, the expensive ones, even though I was eleven, too old for spades and buckets.

Now you've fallen asleep, your breathing deep and regular and your head on my arm. I love your head. I know your head well. If I were sitting behind you on a train, and I didn't know you were on the train, I would recognize you by your hair, the way it shapes into itself like that on the back of your head. I feel the weight of your head on me. We have come so far. It frightens me to think how far we have come and how fast we've gone, how little we've noticed of it. I swear on this gravity in the dark that from now on I will take small steps, I will take care, I will look at each indifferent rock, notice each leaf I pass with you.

Then I fall asleep, still wearing all my clothes. When I wake up it's morning and you are already awake, up and dressed and ready to go. You smile at me; your face is closed and fresh.

Come on, you say.

It's another day. There are three galleries to see before five o'clock. We had better get moving.

miracle survivors

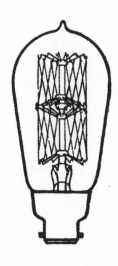

When the thaw set in they found one man still alive who'd been buried in the snow for over a week. His skin was blue and his pulse so submerged that the man from the rescue services almost missed the beat altogether and took him for dead. His clothes were stuck to his skin under his arms and at his chest and neck and crotch.

In town that year the snow had reached over two foot high and out of town had lain thicker than most living people could remember. The main news on television, between the sports results and the *Generation Game*, ran a report about the white Christmas there was going to be in the Highlands, and the radio said not to travel, and if you had to, to carry a spade in the boot of your car.

Several people had suffocated in their cars trying to keep warm with the ignition left on, snow piling round them on the gone roads, snow creeping up the windscreens and blotting the windows out. One couple, found sitting in the front seats with their arms frozen round each other, looked like they'd just fallen asleep. The bodies of other people surfaced near their abandoned cars as the slow work of the thaw went on. But the old man, still breathing, just, they found by chance at the side of the Culloden road while they were searching for somebody else. Nobody on the list of people missing matched his description. Well that's no surprise now, is it? he said to the nurse afterwards. It's not as if I told anyone I was planning to be missing now, did I?

Macpherson, Thomas, she wrote on the form. She wrote Not Known in the spaces marked date of birth and next of kin. She wrote the word Traveller in both the space marked occupation and the space marked address. I've been all over, the man told her hoarsely as she wrote. I've been to Iceland, I was there once and you know there wasn't any dark at all. It was all daylight. I'm not making that up. I had a bath in a hot spring. What's your name? Well Margaret, it was fine and warm under the snow, Maggie, is it Meg you get called, it had the makings of a fine bed, if you'd only been there yourself to keep me warm. Don't get me wrong now, I'm not meaning anything by it, just a thought, and a polite thought, and a very nice one too.

The nurse told the reporters what his first words had been when he came round: No Wonder. *No Wonder Says Miracle Survivor. He wanted to say something so I put my head to his ear to hear and he whispered the words "no wonder" to me, said Nurse Margaret Gallagher (22).* Afterwards, when he was well enough to be photographed, the old man explained that it wasn't wonder he'd said, it was vinegar: No Vinegar. He'd been in the ditch and dug himself down in the snow to make room, and where he was digging, he said, he'd found a half-eaten bag of chips someone must have thrown out of a car window on to the verge.

Can you describe to us how it felt under the snow? the reporters asked.

Oh, it was fine and dandy, the man said. I had a good rest.

The papers sent their photographers back to take his picture again, this time still wrapped in the tinfoil hospital blanket and holding a fish supper. My father's father, he told the photographers, knew a lad that went down on the *Titanic*. My father's father went through two fortunes. My father's father would have had enough to go on the *Titanic* himself if he'd wanted, the man said.

By the end of the week the nurses were squabbling over who'd get to put the lotion on, who'd get to shave him, who'd get to do his feet. One day one of them showed him a photograph of her boyfriend. Oh he's a handsome young stag, the old man said, you'll have a herd of big-eyed bairns out of him and you'll be together for a long time, look at him, he'll live to be a hundred years and be loyal to you for more than seventy.

The next day all the nurses, even the men, and some

from the other wards, were in and out of his room showing him their photographs.

The younger nurses took to sitting on the edge of his bed whenever they had a break; the Sister gave three of them a dressing-down about it one morning, going in there on the thinnest pretext just dodging their work and making more work for others. The nurses looked at the ground so as not to look at each other; she'd be angrier if any of them was to laugh now. But the Sister leaned forward and spoke in a quite different voice. Has he told any of you what it was like, what it was really like being under there all that time? Does he remember anything about it? She looked from one kirby-gripped white-hatted head to the next; they were sitting up, looking up now, they all spoke at once. Has he said at all how they actually came to find him in amongst all that snow? the Sister asked, low, insistent.

It was the tree he broke the branch off, Shona said. He says the snow was so high, Sister, that he could just reach up and break the branch off, and all the snow from the other branches shook down on to him and nearly knocked him over, nearly buried him there and then, he says, but he stuck the stick as far as he could through the snow into the ground and tied a bit of his coat on to it.

Oh, the Sister said. Sort of like a flag, do you mean?

The others told the Sister their versions of the story. Just ask him, Sister, just ask him yourself, he'll tell you, Shona said. Shona was especially fond of Tom. Shona means great beauty, he'd told her. To everything there is a season, Shona, and you'll have three babies, three girls, and they'll each go through their lives like nobody else in the world and make you happy, so they will, mark my words. And at the new year, be sure and not lend anybody anything or pay anybody anything you owe them. You'll end up lending and paying all year. Whatever else you do lend no one your matches, and don't be taking rubbish out of the house. The things you do on New Year's Day make your luck for the rest of the year, now, so make sure your first-foot is tall and dark and very handsome. I'll be your first-foot this year, shall I, eh Shona?

Shona pulled one of the decorations down off the wall and wrote her address on the back of a piece of paper chain.

Later that week Sandra (noble beauty) and Fiona (fine boned and prosperous) were tucking him in, one on each side, when he said, I'll be needing my clothes back now.

They looked at each other across the bed. You're not fit to go yet, Tom, Fiona said. Your clothes are burnt, Tom, Sandra said. We'd to send them for burning. And we'd to cut them off you anyway, you couldn't have put them on again even if they hadn't been burnt.

What about my boots? the man asked.

Against the wishes of the doctors, in the clothes of the fathers and brothers of nurses and with folded pound notes in so many of his pockets, the man left the hospital on the last day of the year.

*

Twenty minutes to midnight, twenty years later, and Dawn is about to break in to a newsagent's on the deserted station concourse. Not break in exactly, since they have a key though they're not sure what it's for. This girl Tina who Dawn's been hanging about with for the past while for safety in numbers lifted it off one of the men who run the shop when she was doing him a favour earlier. Tina swears she's seventeen though Dawn suspects she's nearer fifteen. Anyway Tina's favours have been keeping them warm all week. Tonight it's freezing cold again, too cold for snow.

It's weird to see the station so empty. There's nobody down there, not a soul, just them and the great scuffed space of the floor shining from the lights left on in the shops, their windows all cheap with tinsel. The front of the newsagent's has a metal shutter down. Tina rattles the padlock then looks around as the sound echoes across the concourse. Round the back in the dark they try the delivery door and the key turns. The door has a panel that's been blocked off by a big plank of wood; someone's tried breaking in here before.

Tina makes straight for the Mars Bars. Behind the counter Dawn finds a convector heater and switches it on with her foot. She puts her face in the blast of air as it warms, and her hand by a telephone under the counter. She picks the receiver up. She listens to the dialling tone.

Can't be new year yet, she says. There's no crossed lines.

In the light from the display window she fills her pockets with packs of cigarettes, and she tries the till, just to see, but it won't open. She chooses a box of matches with care, and sits on a stack of newspapers while she lights a cigarette. She looks at Tina, sitting on the floor in her dirty pink jacket with the *Broons* annual open in her hands and all the racks of magazines behind her.

Princess Tina, Dawn says, and blows smoke out and up.

Tina looks at her blankly. Throw me them, she says. The matches and all.

You're too young, Dawn says. It's bad for you.

Tina has a list of swears the like of which Dawn has never heard before, not even in any of the places she's been over the last few months. Tina sounds like she's from Glasgow though Dawn's not very good at accents; she could be from anywhere down here. I'll bet she's Glaswegian, though, Dawn thinks. I mean, she really knows stuff, even if she is younger than me.

The swears stream through the air at Dawn until the cigarettes land at Tina's feet. And the matches, Tina says.

Dawn reaches behind the counter for a new box and throws them over. Tina bends the *Broons* annual open on her knee to keep her place, lights a cigarette.

Did you ever read that one when you were wee, Dawn says, where they have these posh people coming round for tea and the mother is all up to high doh about the state of their house and the posh people seeing it? The one where they all have to stand in a funny way, like the tall one has to stand with his hand covering the damp patch on the ceiling and one of the girls has to lean against the wall with her elbow to cover something else, and someone else has to stand on the patch that's in the carpet? That's a really funny one.

Tina doesn't look up. On the front cover of the book there's pink-purple pretend tartan; the Broons are gathered for a family portrait. In yellow, the words say Scotland's Happy Family. It's not even the real Broons any more, Dawn thinks, Daphne's supposed to be uglier than that. She feels dull suddenly, like something angry in a dark tweed coat is thudding itself at her from behind a wall of misty glass or ice. On the back cover, the Bairn is asleep on Paw's lap in a big chair.

They always have one about new year on the very last page, Dawn says.

Tina flicks to the back and reads the page hard. Aye, she says eventually, so there is.

Dawn stubs out the cigarette on the papers she's sitting on. The date she stubs the cigarette out near is December 31st. All over the front are the things that have happened over the last year. People who've been shot or killed. OJ. That house where they buried those girls. Princess Di. Dawn puts another cigarette to her mouth, looks around the shop. There's so much stuff in here. Cold drinks and books and all those magazines, sweets and chocolate and postcard racks and batteries and things for cameras, and things for tourists, tartan things, fluffy white dogs wearing tam o'shanters, dolls dressed up as pipers. She wipes the ash and picks the black burnt bits off the top newspaper, smooths down the burnt place with her hand.

Tina is coughing hard. After she finishes she says, is it new year now?

I think so, Dawn says. She looks at the inside of the silver metal shutter over the front of the shop. I wonder who'll first-foot us, she says. Tina laughs, and coughs. She always coughs like that when she gets in somewhere warm.

What were you doing this time last year? Dawn asks.

Jesus Christ, *I* don't know, Tina says, and looks at Dawn as if she's said something really stupid. She lies back on the splay of shiny covered magazines; she looks like women do when they lie back in luxurious baths on adverts on tv.

No, Dawn says. It's important. What you do on New Year's Day makes your luck for the whole year.

Tina sits up. I know what we could do, she says.

What? says Dawn.

We could phone our horoscopes, Tina says.

For the next while they listen to long messages on the ends of the numbers they find in the women's magazines. Tina is Sagittarius, Dawn is Leo. They are both going to have a year filled with changes in their careers and on the domestic front. Tina phones a thing she calls the itching line and they hold the phone between them to hear an oriental-sounding man telling her she will meet her master in the street, and that two mountains sit between her and the future.

Aye, Tina says, that'll be right.

Then Tina closes her eyes and punches in a number at random. It rings at the other end, and someone answers. Happy new year, Tina shouts down the phone. Happy new year from Tina and Dawn.

She does this three or four times. It's Tina, she says to one person. Dawn can hear it's a man's voice. *Tina*, Tina says. From that party. I'm really hurt you don't remember me.

At another number there's someone playing the pipes at the tinny other end of the phone; happy new year, they both scream, happy new year, a lot of people at the other end shout. Tina gets them to tell her the address. That sounded like a good laugh, she says to Dawn.

Yeah, Dawn says. She gives the receiver to Tina, pushes it to Tina's ear as she presses a combination of numbers for her. Then she steps back, goes over to the magazine racks and watches from there.

Hi, Tina says to the voice that answers. Happy new year. It's Tina. Don't you know me? It's Tina and her friend –

She looks over at Dawn, sees Dawn's face.

It's Tina and her friend Denise, she says. No, never mind, you won't, it's been a long time. We're just calling to wish you a very happy new year. All the best for ninety-six. And many more of them and all. Cheers now. Bye.

Tina puts the phone down.

Who answered it? Dawn asks.

A woman, Tina says. She didn't know who we were or anything. I told her happy new year from both of us.

Then Tina and Dawn spend half an hour spelling out, in tubes of peppermints and packets of chewing gum across the floor of the shop, the words HAPPY NEW YEAR FROM THE SEXY SUPER MODELS WE WERE HERE BUT YOU WERE NOT YOUR LOSS. They stand back to look at what they've written. They tidy the magazines back on to the shelves and keep the ones they want to take with them. With chocolate and more cigarettes in their pockets, with their magazines and with one of the disposable cameras from the peg above the lottery machine, they lock the door behind them and head for the party with the pipes that they heard down the other end of the phone.

Morning is coming up now, grey and clear. As they go along the road they take photos of each other and of the people who drunkenly pass them. One man has his photo taken with his arm round Dawn, calls her darling and gives her a fiver when she asks. When the roll of pictures jams to an end in the camera Tina tosses it over a hedge into someone's garden. Well, she says, that's what they're for, you're supposed to throw them away.

They link arms, laughing. All the way down the road, looking for an address that Tina's not sure she remembers right, they laugh about how the man who runs the newsagent's in the station will be getting the biggest phone bill he's ever had, and what he'll think when he gets into his shop and finds their message, and how he'll remember it every new year, maybe be telling his customers and his family and friends all about it for years and years to come.

the theme is power

The thing is, I really need you with me in this story. But you're not home. You won't be home for hours yet.

I stand about in the kitchen for a while, not knowing what to do about it, because the story is right at the front of my head, and I decide to do something, I decide to do the dishes. They need done anyway (three days' worth) and what's more, with my back to the table standing at the sink I can imagine you, sitting up on it with your legs swinging, eating an apple. So. Listen to this. This is what happened.

It starts with Jackie and I standing at a bus stop in Trafalgar Square. (So it happened quite long ago? you say behind me.) We had taken our rucksacks off; she was sitting on hers and I was leaning on mine, and we were tired and happy, nearly home from a little travelling, still excited by being in such a famous square in such a big city even if we were only there for the half hour it would take to catch a bus.

A woman came over. She was wearing a headscarf tied tightly round her head. This was strange because it wasn't raining, it was mild and clear though it was dark, an evening in late September just after nine o'clock.

Her mouth was a straight set line in her face. Hello girls, she said.

Hello, we said.

Have you just arrived in London? she said.

We told her we'd just got back from Paris, we'd gone there on a Magic Bus special fare of only £7.00 return and now we were catching the nine-thirty bus on our way to stay with my sister who lived with her four sons and her husband near Reading before we went up home tomorrow to Scotland. That was where we were from, Scotland, and not just Scotland but right up in the north of Scotland. We told her all this, detail after detail, without being asked. When one of us had told her one detail, the other would come in with something else. We were charming. We'd have told her anything. I think we must have felt privileged that a stranger had chosen us to speak to out of all the millions of people in London. But more: she'd looked unhappy, and that was a shame.

It's very late to be travelling, she said. You must be tired, coming all that way. Wouldn't you rather stay here in London for the night? I have a flat you could stay in, just for tonight. It's free, you wouldn't have to pay, since it's only for one night. You look like nice girls. My flat is right above Miss Selfridge. That's right in the middle of Oxford Street.

I nodded. I knew where Miss Selfridge was, because I had been to London before on a weekend break with my parents and our hotel had been just off Oxford Street, a moment round the corner from the Miss Selfridge shop.

You see, the woman said, interrupting me. You could go shopping in Oxford Street tomorrow morning if you want, and then you could catch the bus to your sister's. It's a very nice flat. There's plenty of room, it's very roomy, and I live there by myself.

We both said what a good place that must be to have a flat.

Yes, she said. I've got a stereo, and hundreds of records. Lots of the latest ones, practically everything that's in the charts. I could give you a lift. My car's just over there.

We thanked her very much and I said that my sister was expecting us and would already have made us something to eat.

Are you sure? she said. My car's just round the corner. Or maybe I could give you a lift to your sister's house. Sometimes the buses don't stop at this stop, you know. Sometimes they miss it out on their way round London, and I'm not busy tonight. You're in luck. I could give you a lift.

Some more people came to wait at the stop. The woman stepped back. We thought she must be very shy. We said goodbye and thanks, and watched her cross the road.

That was kind of her, I said to Jackie.

Yes it was, Jackie said. It was nice of her to offer.

I tell you. We stood there, seeing and hearing nothing, myself and Jackie, my best friend, my first true love, below a rumbling rockfall, an avalanche that would have buried us, swallowed us stonily up. We must have looked about fourteen or fifteen to that woman, small and adolescent-thin. We must have looked like we'd run away from somewhere. Naive, bedraggled, in unwashed clothes after a week in the cheap hotels of Paris with their toilet floors all cracked linoleum and scuttling beetles, the woman at the reception desk grinning so we couldn't not stare at the gap where her front teeth had been and telling us, yes I know, I know, one bed is better for you girls, also it does not cost so much and that is also a good thing, yes? We had looked young enough to get in for nothing at the Louvre and to pay only half price on the tube when we got back to London, even though in reality we were nearer twenty. In guilt-stricken love with each other for just over a year by then, a year of pure fumbling and ecstasy; I don't use the word lightly, we knew all about purity. We were high and pure as Michael Jackson's child self singing *I'll Be There*, and we knew about things like loneliness and longing, and how to hide them, how to hide our sadnesses and kindnesses. We believed in the superiority of feeling, and we believed there had to be some superiority in everything we felt since we felt it so strongly in the face of such taken-for-granted shame. I can still see our heads together, our eyes and our mouths, intent and pretty and serious as stoats, as we thought things as innocent and perilous as, for instance, that suicide must be a good thing, at the very least a truly romantic thing, something all truly romantic people would do, since people so clearly felt so much when they did it.

You know what I think? Jackie said as we watched the woman in the headscarf cross the square away from us. I think that poor woman is a very lonely person.

I didn't want to be outdone on the superior understanding of feeling. Yes, I said, yes, and a very sad person too.

We nodded sagely. The bus drew up. We loaded our rucksacks on, and the bus circled Nelson's Column, and we saw from the bus window the same woman with the headscarf leaning out of the window of her car, and behind her in the car there was a man with a thick black beard. This man was so huge, so looming, he took up nearly all the back seat. She glared up at us out of the window, and as the bus pulled away we saw the man getting out of the back of the car and running round to the driver's seat.

They were there behind the bus all the way through the city and then all the way along the motorway. We watched them out of the back window; we saw their faces below us every few yards, distorted under light and glass when we passed under the streetlamps. After three quarters of an hour we couldn't be sure if they were still coming; they weren't directly behind the bus any more. When the bus stopped to let us off in the dark outskirts of the village where my sister lived,

Jackie stood at the wheel and, near breathless with fear, told the bus driver about the people following us.

So? the driver said. He shrugged his shoulders. The bus door hissed shut and left us on the verge.

We abandoned the rucksacks, left them lying. We stumbled three hundred yards along a main road so unlit that I remember the grass of the verge as black. We found the passageway to my sister's street, and when we got to her house we hammered on the door and stammered it all out on the doorstep about the woman and the man. My sister's husband phoned the police while we drank tea and ate toast and sat dazed and safe in front of their television watching *What The Papers Say*, but I could tell from the tone of his voice, embarrassed and explanatory in the hall, that he thought we were overreacting, or maybe even making it up.

So that's the first part of the story. I put my hand into the water below the foam and feel for the cutlery, try not to lift out sharp knives by their blades, and even now it makes me shake my head a little, like I would if I woke up and opened my eyes and found I couldn't focus properly; even now after all this time it terrifies me, what might have happened to us if we'd been good enough or docile or hopeless enough to have gone with that woman, when she asked, to her nice flat above Miss Selfridge.

You see, this is what I mean. I believed, and somewhere in my head I still believe, that this flat existed. Of course there wasn't a flat there at all, or if there was, it certainly wasn't hers. But all the horrors, all the things I don't want to imagine, still take place in that muffled flat, above the lit-up window displays and the darkened shop floor, the rows and rows of clothes, the silent accessories of the year 1979 and the late-evening traffic roaring past at random on the street outside.

The other thing is, my father is here visiting. I forgot to tell you. He's why I began thinking about all this. Here, he said to me earlier when we were having our lunch at the art gallery, do you remember that time you and your other friend, what's her name, were at that bus stop and that woman tried to get you into her car?

He's asleep through the front. He just turned up. I don't know how long he's staying this time. This morning I was reading a book and he arrived at the front door. Never mind that, he said. Come on. Let's go out. I'll take you out for your lunch. Where's your friend? Out? Never mind. Let's go.

You wouldn't have caught him dead in an art gallery when I was a child. Then after we'd been a few times I realized that he wants to go there specifically so he can say things like: What's that then? what's it called? *A Woman's Face?* well it doesn't look like a woman's face to me, it looks like a dog's dinner, unless she's really ugly in which case she should get surgery, you know, plastic surgery, *A Woman's Face*, is that her nose? is it? God help her, I could do better than that and I can't even paint, she'd have been better off with me painting her. And what's that? what's the point of that? *Boulder*

In Room. A boulder in a room? a picture of a boulder in a room? eh? that painter's got his sizes all wrong, his perspective, how would that size of boulder have got into that room? that boulder would never have, it's too big, the room's too small, he'd never get it through the door, you'd have had to build the bloody house round the boulder to get a boulder that big into the room.

I used to explain, laboriously and painedly, about cubism and surrealism and modernism and seeing things from different perspectives. Then I realised I was being patronizing and irrelevant, and that he wasn't listening anyway. It's much better now when we go. This morning we had a really nice time. We walked round all the rooms so he could say the things and I could nod and listen, and after that we went to the art gallery cafeteria.

I don't know if I've ever told you this story about my father before. When I was about nine, one summer evening I was out playing by myself, kicking around in the cinders behind the garages, and I saw a man. He was sitting in the empty square of space and rubble where a garage had been, and holding his hand down low he said, can you see? Yes, I can see, I said. I thought the man must be stupid. I wasn't blind. Then I saw that what he was holding, what he wanted me to look at, was his penis. I looked at it for a while like I was supposed to, then I waved my hand at him to say good-bye and strolled back to our garden with my hands in my pockets, rather pleased with myself, a little cocky you might say, about what I'd seen. My father was cleaning our car outside our garage. I told him about the man. Dad, guess what? I said.

I had never seen him be so lithe, move so fast. He threw down the sponge; it splashed into the bucket and sent the water slopping out over the ground. A moment later, with me falling further behind him in the mob of children drawn by the noise of something happening, there he was, my father, several strides ahead of the group of other fathers he'd gathered from the houses, and all of them racing across the field after a man who was right at the other side of it. When they reached him my father was the first there and the first to punch him down. I wasn't sure if it was the same man, but it didn't matter; all the fathers stood in a ring round him until the police came to take him back to the mental hospital, which was only half a mile away across the canal and was where he was an in-patient, the man they'd beaten. My father was a local hero for weeks after that, for months. People from the street where we lived then would probably still remember the night; it had an air of celebration, like Bonfire Night, or like the night when John Munro's father took his lawnmower and in a stroke of genius mowed a football-pitch-sized square for the first time into the long grass of that field.

I pile the bowls and cups up on each other, a bit unsafe. (Don't you feel bad about that man who got beaten up? you say behind me. Quiet, I say, I'm thinking.) These days my father can fall asleep just about anywhere with the blank ease of, say, a kitten or a puppy; I look around and he's gone again, his head down, his chin on his chest and his breathing heavy and regular. He's fallen asleep through there with the television up quite loud, and I can still hear him sighing out a rhythm over a relentlessly sincere speech of Clinton's. When I went through to collect his cup he was sleeping through footage of dead Iraqi people, a mother and a child lying poisoned where they fell in their village street, their faces bloated. I switched it off. He opened his eyes. Put it back on, he said, I'm watching the news. I switched it back on. There was a graph on the screen showing Clinton's soaring popularity, and a shot of a film star saying, we don't care how much tail he chases so long as he does his job, and my father sighed, closed his eyes and went back to sleep.

(But is it connected? I'm a bit lost, are they connected, the story about your father and the story about the woman with the headscarf? you say behind me. You throw your applecore at the bin with perfect aim; in it goes. Yes, but wait, in a minute, I say. Bear with me.) I'm thinking how my father fell asleep at the art gallery too, after lunch, sitting on a cushioned stool. For a while I stood on the other side of the room and watched him sleeping. Lately he's grown a beard, for what I think is the first time in his life. He looks like a different man, like a salty old seadog, like Sean Connery. He told me proudly earlier about a woman flirting with him in the supermarket. I'm not surprised; he looks better now – is better-looking, is in better shape – than he was ten years ago when his business was folding. He looks a lot better than he did when he was in his mid-fifties even, that much younger than he is now, the age he would have been when Jackie and I arrived back from London full of our story, and full of lies about how we'd slept, how we'd only had one room but there'd been two beds, or how there'd only been one bed so one of us had slept on the floor. But my father and mother were distraught, hardly listened to us; so strained-looking that for the first time in my life I realised they would break; and this was all because someone had sent an unpleasant, unsigned letter to the local tax office about how my father's business was far too booming.

(Aha, you say.) But now I'm thinking of my father's shop, which sold lightbulbs made to look like candles, with pretend plastic wax dripping down their sides and bulbs whose elements flickered like flames. There were dusty stacks of batteries and plugs, and cables of all widths rolled in great reels on steel poles on the wall; there were kettles and irons and mini-fans and hair-dryers, there were drawers of parts and drawers of fuses, drawers filled with anonymous bits of plastic and rubber that could make things work. Behind the counter there were two loose wires, live, for testing lightbulbs; he used to tease me, here, touch these, go on, and sometimes I would, just to get the queasy feeling all over again and to see if it really felt as horrible as I remembered. Propped on the back wall behind and above him was an old piece of cardboard from the nineteen fifties when the shop first opened. On it a dapper-suited man was demonstrating a lamp to an ecstatic woman with the words The Theme Is Power radiating like a rainbow over their heads, and over the head of my serving father, in a lit-up exclamatory arc.

His shop was next door to the Joke Shop, which had black-face soap, electric buzzers for shaking hands, fake dog's dirt and bluebottles and nails-through-the-finger, brandy glasses with the brandy sealed inside the glass so the drinker would be fooled, and special bird-call whistles which my father, whose laugh rang down the streets and round the shops from a great distance away, showed me how to use; how to tuck metal and leather into the roof of your mouth, moisten properly with your tongue, and then you could imitate any bird you heard. It sold x-ray specs, which my mother confiscated from me when she saw the sharp nail-points holding them together next to where the open eye would be.

You see, I tell you. My mother was still alive, and pretty well, when Jackie and I got back with our bus-stop story; but it was the beginning of her worrying herself awake every night wondering which acquaintance, which friend, which familiar face had sent the letter; maybe someone who'd been round for a cup of tea and had sat smiling at her in that very armchair, had complimented her on her kitchen full of shiny electrical things and their house it had taken them nearly forty years to own. It was a terrible time. A man who worked in the tax office, a neighbour, an old friend, came round; he sat on the couch and hung his head. His aftershave was apologetic. He said, usually we get these crank notes, and usually they go straight in the bucket, I'm so sorry, I didn't see it otherwise it would've. My mother patted his hand. My father gave him a whisky, patted him on the back.

(Then what happened? you ask.)

She wasted, became ill. He aged twenty years in one month. He worked with the inspector who came to take his business apart; she was young, a woman in her late twenties, and she found an accountant's old mistake in his books, charged him for that, and when she was finished she shook his hand and said she'd enjoyed her time with him and that enjoyment was a rare thing in her job. Then that was it, over. But my mother sat on a low stool in her kitchen, drinking tea on her own and staring at the food mixer, at nothing, knowing for a fact that someone had wanted to hurt her.

I turn round. You're not there. I knew that. There's no one here, just me, and my father breathing next door.

So I wipe down the table. I wipe the crumbs on to the floor instead of into my hand like I should, and my mother laughs down at me. Now that she's safe in heaven dead she tends to laugh at all the slatternly things I do, all the things that would have enraged her when she was alive. I leave a sheet on the line for two days and two nights, regardless of rain and the judgements of neighbours, and she laughs delightedly. I blow my nose on my clothes and she laughs and laughs, claps her hands. I try sewing anything, anything at all, and she roars with laughter in my ear like it's the funniest thing she's ever seen.

My mother, all her illness gone; holding the soles of her feet and rocking with laughter up there above us. When I was about thirteen, back when I felt scared and guilty all the time, I asked her once if there wasn't anything she'd done in her life that she still felt bad about. She was getting ready to go out to work. Her hand paused by her mouth holding the lipstick, and her face went thoughtful. Yes, she said suddenly, lots of things, and she laughed, then her face fell, she looked crushed, she sat down on the side of the bed. Yes, there was the time someone stole my new shoes and it was my fault, and my mother, your granny, I'd never seen her so angry. We were poor. I've told you before, though you can't imagine what that means. We were poor but your granny always made sure we had shoes, it was a thing of decency for her. So there was one year we got our new shoes for going back to school, but my best friend was barefoot and I wanted to be too. I didn't want to be any different. So I took my new shoes off and I hid them in the grass outside the school, and I was barefoot all day. But when I came out they were gone, someone had taken them. It was terrible. It was the end of the world. I had to go home to my mother with no shoes.

She sat on the bed with the wardrobe door open opposite her, and she waved her hand over all the shoes, hundreds of shoes hardly scuffed, piled several-thick inside each other and on top of each other on the wardrobe floor. Look at that now, she said. Then she lifted the hairspray tin and shook it. This'll chase you, she said. Off you go you monkey, I'm going to be late because of you, or if you're staying, cover your eyes and take a deep breath, I'm going to spray.

(I still don't really get the connection, you say.) Well, no. Okay. Actually you don't say anything, you're not home yet. But you'll be home soon, so I imagine your key in the door, you kicking off your shoes and hanging your jacket in the hall, and coming through, stealing up behind me and kissing the back of my neck. Your face will be cold, and when I turn to kiss you back, your nose will be cold and you'll taste of outside. You'll say, you're doing the dishes, what's happened, has the world changed? is someone here? is your father here? your father must be here. You'll point to the drying crockery. You'll stand back to admire its pile-up, like people admiring art. Brilliant, you'll say. Pure sculpture.

You always say something like that.

And then it's later, it's late, it's nearly midnight now, and you're home. You came home half an hour after I finished the dishes. Now my father is in bed in the spare room. I can hear him snoring all the way through two walls. It's disturbing, as usual. It's too familiar.

I'm lying in bed. You're tired; you're not saying much. You didn't say much at supper. I think you might be in a bad mood. You undress, folding your clothes as you take them off.

I'm a little worried for my father. It can be cold in

the spare room; I should have given him a hot water bottle. I think of his shop, dark and gone. The last time I passed it, it had become a clan heraldry shop, its windows full of little shields; a bored-looking man sat behind the counter and there were no customers. I think of the art gallery today, and the picture we saw with the massive rock in the room and the door blocked behind it. My head full of dark thoughts, I think of Jackie again, of how finally we betrayed each other, fell out of love, in love with others; we couldn't not.

I stop thinking about it all. It's too sore.

Outside someone goes past, a drunk angry man, and it sounds like he's hitting the cars parked along the road with a stick or his fist. He's shouting. I'm doing your fucking cars, he shouts. You better come out and get me. None of yous will. You're all fucking cowards. I'm going to do all your fucking cars.

His voice fades as he moves down the road. You get into bed. You switch the bedside light out, and we're in the dark. You sigh.

Listen, I say, and I want to tell you the whole story, but it rolls around dangerously in my head. So I say,

What if there was a great big boulder in the room, and you've no idea how it got in, it's so much bigger than the door.

What? you say. You turn beside me, speaking into my back.

A boulder. It's nearly as big as the room, I say. And it's slowly coming towards you –

Towards me? you say.

Towards us, I say, and it's crushing all the things in the room.

It'd better not, you say. We haven't paid this bed off yet, I'm not having it destroyed by a stupid, what is it, boulder?

But listen. What if there was a great big stone in the room, I say, big enough to almost be up to the ceiling, and as wide as from there to there.

A stone, you say sleepily. As big as the room. Coming towards us. Where's my chisel? get me a chisel, find something we can use as a hammer. You'd pay a fortune for that much rock at a stonemason's.

Under the covers you take my hand and turn it around, put your fingers through mine, interlocked, and you fall asleep like that, holding my hand.

That's all it takes. One glance, one sidelong blow from you, and a rock as big as a room explodes into little bits of gravel. I pick around in the shards of it, remember someone I saw today in the art gallery, a stranger, a man who sat down next to my sleeping father with such care, trying not to wake him. I remember my father like he was way back then, showing me the inside of a plug and which colour went where; and I think of my father now, flirting with a woman in a supermarket, playfully circling each other in the checkout queue. I make the woman very good-looking, to please him, and a little like my mother, to please us both. I remember the man I saw all those years ago in the space where the garage had been, cradling his

137

genitals like he was holding a creature, something new-born, furless; and the fathers, stupid with protection, hurling themselves along the backs of the houses; and my mother telling me to shield my eyes so the hairspray chemicals wouldn't get in them. And then I think back to Jackie and me in London waiting at that bus stop, two teenage girls in a random city, good enough to believe the lies that a stranger told, even caring in the first place that a stranger might be sad.

You're next to me asleep with my hand still in yours, my father is snoring along the hall, and I'm not long from sleep myself. I lie in our unpaid bed and trust you, carelessly, precariously, with my whole heart. That's the story finished, that's all there is to it. One last time though, before I lock the door on it for the night, turn the sign from Open to Closed, I picture Jackie, wherever she is, wherever she might be in the world.

I imagine she's holding such a hand. I imagine her safe and sound.

instructions for pictures of heaven

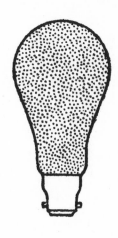

The woman in the fruit shop has a face like bruised fruit. If you sit here on the benches outside the Co-op people think you're unemployed. That makes some people ignore you and some people stop to sit beside you. Some of them are mad, the ones who pass as well as the ones who stop and sit down. You can pretty much tell by their faces. Your instinct is getting good now for telling which is which. When they walk past and ignore you it is easier to look properly at their faces. Whereas, if someone is sitting beside you talking to you and you look him or her (usually him) in the face then he thinks you're looking at him for some reason like you want something or you fancy him or you want to give him something or tell him something. You have to be careful.

It doesn't even matter if you only sit on the bench for a minute. People who see you there still think what they like about you. It's the same if you stand about outside anywhere in the middle of town, if you're waiting for someone, or especially if you squat down on the pavement or sit on a step because you're tired. Then people look away because they think you're going to ask them for money. Some even give you money even though you're not asking for it. You'd be rubbish on the street. You wouldn't know what to do.

It's busy. It must be lunch hour. They've started selling barbecued chicken in the Co-op. The Co-op Local is its new name. Last year it was called the Stop 'N Shop, and before that it was called the 8 'til Late. Before that it was called something else, you can't remember. Anyway you are quite pleased with yourself for remembering as much as you do about the names of it. A lot of people go past here all the time, and probably none of them remembers about the other names, or even notices about them changing like you notice.

You stretch your toes inside your shoe. Your shoes are new, to you, and not quite the right size; you need a heelgrip or something. A child goes past and it has a face like a frog. A woman goes past and her face is like a plank of wood. A younger woman goes past; she has a face like she is supposed to have, all in the right place, that is what young women are supposed to look like, like someone out of Kays' Catalogue except in a bad temper. An old man goes past. He goes past most days when you're here. His face is lined and grey like the trunk of a tree. He smiles at you and more lines break all over his face. He goes so slowly past you that it is like his smile is in slow motion.

You can watch the faces, there are always more of them. Or you can watch the car registration plates. NEG negative. ARG argument. Or argh (but argh is not a real word). BKL buckle. VVE revive. ELR – yes, ELR elevator. DTF doubtful. NEW new. PEW phew. But maybe phew isn't a real word either. PEW periwinkle. Or just PEW pew. Good. The people on the gameshow on tv who have to do something like this, when Derek the Computer gives them the letters, don't win money, they win dictionaries or holidays at a health farm so it isn't really worth it. You know it is going to be a bad day on the days when you can't keep up with the letters going past on the cars.

Or you can choose to look up. Today the clouds are thick and unbroken though you don't think it will rain. Nuages. That was the French word for it at school. New ages, the sky full of them. It is nearly the end of the century. It is amazing how nearly the end of the century it is. The end of the century will be a brilliant excuse for everybody to get drunk and go mad for a whole year. Or maybe two years, since it said in the paper once that they weren't sure which was the right year to celebrate the end of the century and the new age.

Clouds are particles of ice or water held in the air above ground level. You were good at geography. Cirrus, stratus, cumulus. They sound like magic words but in reality they are just the names of clouds. Cumulo-nimbus is like smoke. Cumulus-humilis, those are the ones like shreds of something in the sky, that can change their shape in seconds.

143

You watch them move above you, a mass of old grey wool.

It must be pretty good though, to work on this side of the road. Better than working on the other where you would never get the sun. Which is what the woman in the fruit shop said to you once, one day when it was sunny. You never get the sun on this side of the street. There is a song about that. It is quite good to think that thing about her having a face like bruised fruit, since she actually sells fruit. Today it looks like someone has really punched her. It particularly looks like someone has been hitting her, because she is pretending so hard that it doesn't matter, that she is just having a day at work, though she is avoiding the eyes of the people who buy things from her and refusing to smile back if they smile at her, and when anyone speaks to her, from the way she is holding herself, it looks as though she is frightened of their words. The pavement outside her shop is covered in boxes of withered-looking flowers. Some days she waves to you, but today you are careful not to look at her when she might see you looking. Her face is a nice face.

You see your own blank face flash before you twice on the shiny moving windows of a car. LFL lawful. SEG. AMR. UAV. TVK.

You watch the faces and clouds and keep your eye out for the words. Some words you get, others you don't.

What's your name? the old lady says.

Gayle, says Gayle.

You're not from round here, the old lady says.

No, I suppose that's right, I'm not, Gayle says and laughs politely.

No, the old lady says. I knew you weren't.

The front door has a bell in the centre with a piece of paper heavily sellotaped over it. Below the sellotape are words: NOT WORKIN. Gayle follows the old lady through the house. The old lady is so small it is like following a small square child. It is hard to tell if it's that she's fat or if it's the number of layers of clothes she's wearing.

The smell of old things gets stronger as they go from room to room. There are photographs everywhere, some framed, some pinned, curling off the walls. In the first room they go through there are piles of clothes everywhere, and there is junk all over the room at the back. It smells like a charity shop. Through the corridor the narrow cracked kitchen is all dishes and dirt, and smells of old animals. It's good of you to help me Gayle, the old lady is saying. Gayle tells her it's no bother at all. She is careful not to touch any surfaces.

Gayle, Gayle, the old lady says as she works at the back door with the key. It's a nice name that, Gayle. I can't do it any more, it's too big for me to move. And after you've taken it round, come back and I'll give you a piece of chocolate.

No no, Gayle says laughing, that won't be necessary. I mean I won't need a piece of chocolate. Don't you worry about any chocolate.

I used to work for a minister and his wife was called

Gayle, the old lady says. He was a minister. I used to clean the house for them up Alpha Road. They were from Whitby. Have you heard of that Whitby? I used to like the sound of Whitby when I used to draw maps. Like Whitsun.

Was that what you used to do when you were young, map drawing? Gayle asks.

Oh yes, when I was a girl, I used to draw maps, the old lady says. She is breathless, still pushing and twisting her hands at the key in the door. There is a line of dirt like a bracelet round one of her wrists.

So where is it you want me to take it? Gayle asks. Shall I take it right round to the front door?

Panic crosses the old lady's face. Oh no, she says. Not right round to the front. I'll never get it back if you take it all the way round to the front. You just take it to the end of the lane. Then the men empty it. I can get it back if you just leave it at the end of the lane.

It'll be a lot easier when it's empty, Gayle says. The smell in the room is overpowering now. She puts her hands on her hips. Then she folds her arms with her hands tucked in.

D'you know, eh, Gayle, I can't get it open, the old lady says.

Here, let me try, Gayle says kindly.

The key gives and turns when Gayle puts her whole weight behind it. The door opens on to an overgrown garden with rubbish in the grass. There is a chicken carcass on the doormat.

Christmas, the old lady says, and kicks it. Look, the

birds have pecked it clean. She laughs. Her laugh
sounds like something falling and breaking.

I'll put that in the bin too, shall I? Gayle says. She
picks up the thin-boned carcass between her thumb and
her first finger. It is unexpectedly light.

You're a good girl, Gayle, the old lady says. And
then come back round for some chocolate.

Gayle tips the bin up on to its wheels. It is quite
hard to push because of the grass being so tangled. A
cloud of mosquitoes flies up out of the grass. Bye now,
she shouts over her shoulder. Maybe see you again.
She pretends she hasn't heard the bit about the
chocolate.

So are you married, Gayle? the old lady calls from
the back door.

Gayle keeps pushing the bin against the lawn. No,
she calls back. Not yet.

You'll still be in school then, the old lady shouts. Her
voice is high and frail.

Gayle laughs. I'm far too old for that, she calls back
over the bin. No, I work in an office.

Oh, an office, the old lady says.

I work in the travel agent's on the Broadway, Gayle
says. Do you know it?

Oh, that'll be good. All over the world, they go, the
old lady says.

But I'm thinking of doing another course, Gayle
says. To get qualifications. There are a lot of courses
you can do.

Oh yes, the old lady says far at the other end of the

garden. You can do a lot of things these days, can't you, hotels or hospitals or anything.

Gayle opens the back gate. The wood of it is rotten.

My name's Marjory, the old woman is calling. But everyone calls me Margie. Call me Margie.

She waves both her hands in the air at Gayle.

Goodbye, Gayle shouts, and waves back.

She pushes the bin up the lane and leaves it at the top by some other bins. She dusts down her hands. She looks at her watch. She has missed two buses.

On her way to the bus stop she passes a boy sitting in the doorway of the post office. He is wrapped in a blanket and there is a dog's head peeping out from beneath the edge. It is a puppy really rather than a dog. Gayle reaches down to pat its head.

He's called Charlie, the boy tells her.

He's lovely, Gayle says.

He's twelve weeks. He's just had his injections, the boy says.

Gayle gives him some money, keeping aside the change she needs for the bus. She doesn't usually give them money, because once she gave money to a man and then she noticed a syringe at his foot, and he saw her notice and tried to kick it out of the way but it was too late, and it was too late for her to get her money back.

She decides not to buy something to eat because she won't be able to eat it anyway until she gets home and washes her hands. She stands in the queue at the bus stop. Behind her, on all the tv screens in the second-hand tv shop window, the African man is on the news again. It is a bit of a joke. Last night he was on the news when he arrived in Britain, because he had come to find the head of an old historic African he was related to, whose head he says was taken by British soldiers who cut off bits of it, like the ears and the lips, and made them into trophies, and put what was left of it in a museum. Everybody had been talking about it at work. He had arrived at Heathrow and had shaken a stick covered in feathers at the customs people. David at work thought it might put people off visiting Africa, which is a real winter moneyspinner and they couldn't afford that to happen at work. But Tony thought it would maybe make more people want to go, because of tradition.

Gayle thinks about her day. This morning she was in a very bad mood, but now she isn't at all. She thinks about the old lady and how she helped her. She tries to remember what the old lady looked like, but she can't. She can't even remember what the boy she's just given money to looks like, though she can remember what his dog's face is like. She looks along the bus queue. Then she shuts her eyes and tries to remember what the people look like and in what order. It is very difficult.

In her head the old lady's face shifts and changes. Her house changes. The smell goes, the dirt goes, the town and time change, and Gayle is looking up at her grandmother, who is dead. But this is a long time before she died, and they are in the white-tiled bath-room in the new council house. Gayle is staying for the weekend. It is a real treat. Her grandmother is showing her how to do magic (it is in the days before fabric softener). She shows her how, if you put the bathroom light out when you're getting undressed to have your bath, and you pull your dress fast enough over your hair and your head, you can make sparks come from nowhere, you can feel the sting of them and if you're quick enough you can even see them round you in the dark.

Gayle smiles to herself. She has done at least two good turns today. She looks away so that no one in the bus queue will see her smiling at nothing. She feels good. She tells herself that probably nobody else in this bus queue today is feeling as good as she is.

1: Women at Work in Jam Factory, circa 1948.

The rumour ran down the line at work, whispered from girl's mouth to girl's ear under the sound of the machines one June morning when the sun threw great slants of light across the machines and over the floor. No, it's true, listen. Why shouldn't it be, when they can send not just voices but pictures with no effort at all all the millions of miles across the world, and when something can happen like Annie Bradley's man walking in like he did after they all thought he was dead and gone, and turning Annie's hair from brown to white in one night? Have you not seen her? Completely white right down to the roots.

One girl knew someone who knew someone who

had seen one of the pictures. She swore on it. The people in them lie about on clouds, with wisps of cloud all round their heads. This woman who had the picture bought it in a studio in London because she had seen her fiancé in it and he was a pilot and was dead, and there he was on a cloud with people all round him, and they were all smiling, though she didn't know any of the people he was with, and she wondered what he was doing with them, all strangers to her.

Grace Chambers laughed out loud when Margie told her it in her ear. I'll bleeding well swear on it too, she said. But she passed on the rumour to the next girl down the line; the next girl was waiting to hear.

Polly sent a note down the line to Margie. Margie tucked it inside her rolled-up sleeve to read when Bithell wouldn't catch her; she was already in trouble. Bithell was down on her for coming in late, it had been such a nice day. But Bithell said maybe Miss Stewart would like to be out in the sun and out of a job too and that this would be easily arrangeable.

Grace stood in front of her so Bithell couldn't see. Polly's note said: Can you get Saturday off? Margie left the line and went up to the glass box.

Who's covering for you on the line? Bithell asked without looking up.

Grace is, Miss Bithell, Margie said. Please, Miss Bithell, can I take Saturday off? A relative is sick and Grace Chambers says she'll work it for me.

Bithell stared at her until she shut the door and backed down the steps.

Measled old toad. Old bitch, face like a clothespeg, like old cheese rind, Margie said under her breath after she turned her back. But it was all right. It'd be all right. She'd written to the telephone exchange for a job. She'd written to a churchman about a house-keeping position. She wasn't going to spend her whole life with her hands bloody well red up to the elbows and stains all over her front and her face. Her hands would be as white as the girls in Labelling. That'd be the life. That'd be the life she'd be having.

2: Debris in Queen Street after bombing, September 1944.

3: Margie and Polly and Vera on the beach at King's Lynn, Spring 1938.

On Friday night Margie left her blue dress out for Polly to wear to London the next day. She pinned the note neatly to the front of it. *See if you see any person I knew in the picture and if you do get it I will get the money some how thanks your a love M.*

Do you think there are special rules for who gets to be in it? Margie said to Grace.

Heaven? Grace said. Christ. You bet there are.

No, Margie said. Do you think, like, people get their photograph taken because they've just arrived? Do you think they have to share a cloud with people they don't even know? Or what if you ended up on the same cloud as her? Margie jerked her head. Above them Miss

Bithell was watching the fruit rolling down the line to be crushed, watching that nobody was eating it.

She's already bought her ticket for her place on the same cloud as you, Grace said, and poked Margie in the side with her elbow. Nah, the likes of her have a special heaven, where they get glass boxes to sit in so they can masticate away to their hearts' content.

Grace had a filthy mouth because she'd gone out with Americans. When will Poll be back? she said. I want to see these pictures. I'd like to meet the man that took them. He'd be worth a bob or two so he would, he knows his way around the world and that's no lie.

Grace had lost all three sisters the night they blew half of Queen Street away.

4: Faked Picture of Heaven (dated 1947, now a collector's item, an auctionable rarity).

Polly brought back two pictures in the end. They were so small you could hardly see the faces, which were impossible to make out anyway. You could make out the smiling and not much else. The man and the woman who ran the studio where you could buy the pictures of heaven charged 2/6 each, and Polly said there was a sign up saying that they could maybe get one of a person you knew, if you could provide them with details of what the person looked like when he was alive. Polly and Margie actually thought about saving a bit of money and doing that, before it was in the papers that the police had shut the shop down and taken the man and the woman to court after someone who was still alive spotted herself dead in heaven in one of the pictures, and the papers said how the man and woman had been charged with fraud and that the man had been to prison after the first war for it too. The papers said they were fined. So that meant they were maybe still doing the pictures somewhere.

None of the faces looked like anyone they knew. Neither Margie nor Polly could recognize any of the people. Grace looked at the pictures and laughed out loud. The pictures got passed down the line with Polly nervous at the pulper, watching to make sure she'd get them back. But then some girl thought she knew someone in one of them, so Polly said she could have the picture, if she paid her the full 4/ for it.

5: Mother and dad, 1922.
6: Mother and dad and the girls, 1935.
7: Polly in the garden, 1967.
8: Polly and Jack in the garden, don't know when.
9: Mary and Uncle Edward, 1930s.
10: Harold and Margie, 1977.
11: Trevor on Harold's side, 1994.
12: Margie's retirement do at the Labour club, 1982.

When Polly went, in 1977, the picture of heaven with its eight blurred faces looking out of the clouds got left with the rest of her stuff to Margie, her sister, who pinned it up on the wall with all the other photos.

*

13: Fifteen girls at work out the back having a smoke, 1949.

There's Polly. There's Margie. That one three along is Grace Chambers. It's not a good likeness. Margie can't remember all the other names now, all those girls at work back then.

14: Row of shops, 1997.
15: Bus queue, 1997.
16: Old lady asleep in chair with mouth open and television on, 1997.

Instructions for pictures of heaven

First, find a photograph of a crowd. It can be one you've taken yourself or one out of a newspaper. Newspaper is good: anonymous and ethereal. It is preferable to choose a happy-looking crowd, smiling faces: a football crowd or a new year crowd or a crowd at a hanging. Peace breaking out is good, or people waiting to cheer royalty on the balcony. Whichever, you will find you get best results from photographs taken from some distance and from above looking down.

Next, cut round some of the faces with a sharp blade. Choose faces that are poorly defined. Cut roughly around hats and hair. Cut round more than one face if you want; two or three can go down well, but be careful, and certainly don't use more than three. Remember, you risk revealing your original source.

Now fill a small clean tin tray with water. Suspend lens and lighting at angles directly above. Place the cut-out faces on lumps of roughly torn wool. (Five or so of these lumps should fit comfortably, with ample space round them, into your tray.) Timing is crucial here, n.b..

Gently and swiftly place the wool on the water. (You may find it useful to ask someone to help with this part of the procedure.) Wait only the second or so it takes for the wool to have absorbed just enough and not too much of the water, enough to weight it still but before it soaks through and destroys the faces. This is the ideal moment to take your picture.

Develop your picture. Pin successful pictures in your window with wedding, engagement and family portraits and the portraits of babies and children. Prepare for your next photograph by returning to stage one (above). Meanwhile, outside your window, crowds will gather peering and pointing. You will hear the shop bell as they push the door open. In wartime particularly, it is guaranteed, you will make a fortune.

kasia's mother's mother's story

The woman is making the sign of the cross. Forehead, chest, left shoulder, right shoulder. She does it again, faster, several times. Her right hand flaps in front of her like a small wing or the head of a snake. Anyone watching will think she is making the sign of the cross.

She is standing in the doorway in the early morning dark. Someone passes, and she looks down. A bicycle rattles past without slowing. The noise of it dies away. Her shoes are still covered in mud. She will never be able to clean it off them. At some point she will need to find a new pair.

But we don't need much, she has been telling her children, combing their hair down with her fingers. We need light. We need air. We need food and water, and to be honest we can do with less of all of these if necessary. And just at this particular time in our lives, we need prayer. What do we need?

Prayer, they both say, the tall one and the small one, good like she wants them to be.

Say the prayers for me, she says. Out loud. That's good. That's very good, my good brave girls. Well done.

Through the nights, through the woods, through the dirt, along the vanishing track in the dark, shifting the smaller one from arm to arm and hauling the other by the hand, she said as loud as she dared and over and over so it became part of the rhythm of the way they moved, the words of the prayers she wants her girls to be able to say. *Pater noster, qui es in coelis sanctificetur nomen tuum. Ave Maria, gratia plena, Dominus tecum.* Come on, say it.

The street is empty again. She crosses the road. They will be safe enough in the room until she gets back, and they have been taught not to speak, and not to say anything to the people downstairs but to be polite, to look friendly and say nothing. The woman downstairs smiled and nodded when she was cleaning her doorway. That means nothing. The door is wedged shut with paper. They are probably still asleep. They will probably still be asleep when she gets back. It will probably be all right. Her shoes are too muddy for the town. She will have to find a way of getting them clean. But it's so early. No one will see.

It is autumn and the air smells of rotting. The whole town smells of it, a smell that doesn't go away, it makes no difference where you are in the town; this side of the river or the other. Here the houses are bigger and the streets are wider. You could look around you and think nothing was wrong. The shops look like they might have things worth selling. That smell at the back of the rotting might even be the smell of a bakery. She stops in front of the church and tries the door. The handle turns but the door won't open.

After she has checked for a back door, and tried the side door built into the wall, she comes back round the front and crosses the road again. This doorway belongs to a dentist. By the church there, there's a bookshop with a metal grille over the window.

Here, her father says to her inside her head.

It's summer, it is a beautiful day, it is her birthday. He has a green book on his desk, he is smiling, and he tosses the book across the room with its pages flown open; she catches it against her chest. *Stories of Chekhov*, bound in green. Down the field by the river there is a good place for reading, a place not too shady and not too hot. Light from the water shimmers the pages. Grass bends by her head. If she just craned her neck she could have the tip of that stem between her lips, in her teeth, she's got it, and she holds the seeds on the end of the stem feeling the rough edges of them against her tongue, and if she is gentle, and careful in the way she moves, and hardly moves at all, she can let the stem go, let it swing back above her forehead and none of the seeds will have broken off.

Stories of Chekhov. She wonders where that book is now. If it is still on the shelf in the back room by the clock that belonged to her mother's mother. If anything is still in its place, where it was left. Who is in the house now. Who has stolen out of it. What things they have taken. She opens her eyes and sees three people going into the church and the door left a little open, and a little open is all she needs.

The dirty walls of the church must once have been white. It smells of damp. It is all long wood seats. She sits on the one nearest the back. The wood is cold through her coat beneath the backs of her legs. There are pictures on the walls. There are statues, and there is a cross at the front; it's too big. A smaller one, a golden one on the table in the middle at the front, looks too expensive. There is a side place with a rail for people to kneel and another statue with another cross. The nun goes past and looks at her. Panic clamps her heart. But the nun doesn't stop. It is all right.

The people are all women, all grim-faced as they go further into the church. She makes her face grim, though her head is lowered, her eyes behind her hair. The priest is dressed in green and white. He stands at the front and raises his arms. They stand up. She stands up.

Forehead. Chest. Left shoulder. Right shoulder.

When they speak she moves her lips. There is no one near enough to hear what she isn't saying. When they change position she does what they do. She blesses the black back of the woman several benches in front who is so old that she moves very slowly, with plenty of warning, from kneeling to standing to kneeling. When they get up and file down to the front she stays where she is, on her knees, with her face behind her hands. She prays very hard. She keeps her eyes shut.

Now there is the smell of something else, smoke. Someone has put out a candle and the smell drifts through the church. Some people think it is enough to bury who you are, to seal it in metal and put it in the ground and remember where it is. This is too dangerous, she knows, so she burned their papers when it was light enough for the flame not to be noticed. She lit the corners one after the other and watched as they blackened and the blackened pieces broke and blew away, and she stamped what was left into the moss. She burned her own first and then the girls', and then her husband's. Before she did this for him she ripped into the parchment with her teeth, and with care, with her cold hands, she tore a ragged path round his name. She put his torn-out name in her mouth and let the old ink, dried for years and all of them his, season after season of him, dissolve into her tongue. She bent down to rub her hands on wet grass to get the ash off them because soon they would be at the town. Her children sat serious, waiting shivering on a log. She smiled. Come on then, she said.

You. Are you all right? Are you unwell?

Her heart fills with blood. She opens her eyes. The mass is over. There is nobody left in the church but when she turns she sees the nun standing far away at the end of the long seat.

Are you unwell? the nun says again.

No, she says, thank you. I'm quite well, thank you.

You look unwell, the nun says. Sit down. Do you need a drink of water?

No, thank you, she says. I'm perfectly fine. Please don't bother.

Stay there, the nun says, still looking at her shoes. Don't move, she says. I'll get you a cup of water.

The nun is gone with the sweeping sound of her clothes. Now all the woman can hear is her own heart. She slides along the seat, opens the buttons of her coat as she moves between the benches, and she leans across the rail at the side, where the robed statue of the lady, its face a little chipped and its eyes lowered, gazes down at the smaller of the crucifixes. The cross is made of wood, it will be light, and it is not too big. She picks it up.

She is over the road with the arms of it pressing into her ribs under her coat, and as she turns on to the bridge, holding it tight to her side with her elbow and slowing herself now, so nobody will think she is going too fast, she imagines the nun coming back with the cup. She imagines her staring at the side rail, knowing something is wrong.

She imagines her angry face, her arms waving in the air as she calls the priest who comes hurrying through, and tells him, and tells him what she's done, what she looks like, what she is wearing, exactly what her hair is like, her nose is like, what colour her eyes are.

She imagines the priest telling the grey-black blur of men, with the nun standing humbly by. She imagines the sound of a swerving car, the footsteps quickening behind her.

Slowly. Walk more slowly.

She thinks of the nun, standing holding the cup of water in the empty church. She imagines the silence round her head like the hollow clanging of bells.

She imagines the nun saying nothing, not saying a word.

When she gets back, they are still asleep. They are exhausted. Soon they will wake up and be hungry. She puts the cross on the mantelpiece in the bare-walled room and sits down at the table. She gets up and moves the cross from the middle to the end, where it can be seen from the door. She sits down again. She puts her head in her hands.

It will help, it will help, it will surely help, it will surely do some good. In fact, it is helping already. Now it will be easier to leave them here while she goes to find something to eat.

a story of love

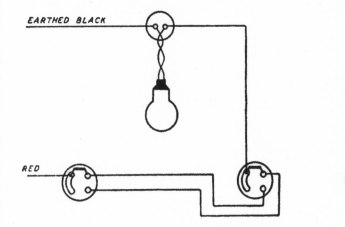

EARTHED BLACK

RED

Tell me a story, I said.

Okay, you said. Any particular kind of story?

A love story, I said since we were in bed and it was November, with the rain dripping through the crack in the drainpipe off the roof on to the old newspapers wadding up the balcony beyond your window, and the wind was wild and rattling the glass, the house was creaking and the world outside was damp and it was cold, the first true chill of winter.

Okay, you said. There was once a boy who really wanted to own a dog.

A boy and a dog, I said. Does it have to be a boy? It's always stories of boys and dogs. Can't it be a girl?

Yes, you said, it can be a girl; true love stories are always interchangeable. There was once a girl who really wanted to own a dog. Actually she would have quite liked a pet of any kind, a fish, a cat, or a bird, but all of these pale into righteous insignificance when you know how much she wanted a dog.

Is this going to be a sentimental story? I said. Is the dog going to die? Because if it is I don't want to hear it.

Listen, you said. Either I tell you a story or I don't. Make up your mind. And you have to promise here and now to take that story on its own terms.

All right, okay. Within reason, I said.

Right, you said. Here goes. There was once a girl etc dog. She really really wanted a dog. But she never did get one. The end.

That's hardly a love story, is it? I said.

Yes it is, you said. It's a story of unrequited love.

But why did she want a dog so much? I said. Why did she never get one? What were the consequences of this thing never happening in her life? Did she die dogless? What happened?

I can't answer all of those questions, you said. But I can tell you that all day long the girl would see dogs with their owners in the streets of the blighted industrial town in which she lived. She would see old people go past with ageing jowly dogs or small yellowing terriers waddling behind them stopping to sniff at the corners of gardens and the edges of fences and walls. She would see ragged travelling people whose sharp-faced dogs wore neckerchiefs instead of collars and were so good they never seemed to need to be kept on a lead, and young well-dressed men with chocolate Labradors, the mouths of the dogs flecked with foam and their eyes rolling, and boys in the park playing

games, throwing chewed sticks for the fierce bull terriers yelping with pleasure and jumping as high as the
boys who owned them. It seemed that everybody else in
the world had a dog but her.

Why didn't she just get one? I asked.

Well, quite, you said. I wonder that too. Because
without one, she was addicted. She took to hanging
around outside pet shops and veterinary surgeries. On
her way home she would go past houses in the early
evening dark, their windows lit up before the curtains
got drawn, and see dogs at the happy feet of couples, or
dogs barking soundlessly behind double glazing, dogs
on couches, in armchairs, with their heads in the laps
of pampering mistresses, dogs on their backs on the
carpet, their paws and ears lolling. She would get home
and go to bed and dream of being the girl in a film she
once saw who befriends a wolf a continent away and
travels the rugged terrain with her wolf dog clawing on
up the mountain track before her, nosing his way
through shallow river rapids with her hand tangled in
the hair on his wet fur back. The end.

That's all very well, I said. But it's not the kind of
love story I wanted. I wanted something different.

You want another kind of love in your story? you
said.

Yes, I said, and I want a story that's a story.

A story that's a story, you said.

A proper story, I said. It was January and minus
twenty outside, the earth frozen and dead, and we were
trying to keep warm under two quilts and it was late,

or rather, far too early, the glowing arms on the clock at half-past four; we had both woken up in the middle of the night. There was work to go to in the morning, we should have been sleeping. I curled myself round your voice.

Right then, you said. There was once a child whose mother fell asleep. The end.

Is that it? I said.

What else do you need to know? you said.

Can't you tell me a little more about them? I said. (I was beginning to despair of your storytelling technique.)

Oh all right, you said. The child was seven or eight, and she was playing by the electric fire. She was walking her fingers in and out round the plastic coals above the bars of the fire as if the coals were a ridge of black hills. She had found that you could unclip the plastic and lift the coals off to see the orange lightbulbs underneath. Her mother had explained to her about how the lights worked, how the bulbs warmed up and sent the steel wheels whirring round so that with the plastic on top it would look like waves of heat were passing through the coals, like real coal. She walked her fingers back and fore through the pretend heat. Her mother had fallen asleep, and the child left the fire and came to the side of the armchair. Her face was level with her mother's sleeping face. She could feel air on her face, and the air came from her mother breathing. She could see her mother's nose and lips move, but only a very little, as she breathed. Her mother's eyes were

closed, and her hair was pretty round them, and somehow she looked as though she were being stern about
something and smiling about it both at the same time.

Your voice had stopped. Is that it? I said.

No, you said, but it's the end of part one. Do you
want part two?

Yes, I said.

Part two, you said, takes place almost thirty years
later. An old woman has fallen asleep in the house
of her daughter, whom she has come to visit. Her
daughter opens the door into the room, bringing her
mother a cup of tea, and finds the old woman in the
chair, her head on one side and her face altered, quite
different, as if she is about to set out on a long and
difficult journey. The daughter sits down in the other
chair with the cup of tea still in her hand. She had come
through with her head full of questions she wanted to
ask her mother, questions about when they were both
younger, when she herself was a child; things she can't
answer, things she needs to know. A moment ago, as
long as it took to fill a cup with water, her mother was
awake, fussing about some flowers on a sideboard. But
now her mother is so soundly asleep that she hasn't
even heard her daughter open the door and come into
the room. She makes a gurgling sound in her throat,
like liquid or mucus has caught in it. Her arm has
slipped off the chair and is hanging down over the
side, swaying slightly as her chest lifts and falls. The
daughter notices how long it seems between each
breath her mother takes. She lifts the cup to her own

mouth and drinks the tea for her mother, so it won't
go cold.

I suppose that's the end of that story, is it? I said
after the silence.

But then I heard your breathing, and realized you
had fallen asleep too.

I lay in the dark and worried that the old lady would
die in her sleep and leave the daughter. I worried for
the child playing so close to a fire and her mother
asleep. I thought back to the story of the dog girl. I
made up lists of reasons why the girl couldn't have a
dog. Perhaps she was allergic to animals and would
swell up like a balloon, unable to breathe, if the oily
dust hidden between the hairs of a dog got anywhere
near her skin. Or someone in her family a long time
ago had been mauled to death by a dog. Or, simply,
dogs weren't allowed in the block of flats where she
lived. Recklessly I imagined a dog for her, I pictured
her getting a dog at long last. Then I worried that
having a dog would mean that she didn't have those
beautiful dreams about the wolf she befriends, and that
the dream wolf, too tamed for the wild, too wild to be
loyal to anyone but the girl he loved, would be left
behind alone, running back and fore at the edge of a
river too rough for him to cross.

The half-stories haunted me. I wanted more of them.

Half-stories? you said. Is that what you think?

It was March and still cold, though right now down
in the garden the crocuses were shivering under a clear
and starry sky and in a few hours the dead tree behind

the houses would be a tree of birds, rising and settling and calling.

Half-stories, you said. Well, that's fine. No, it's absolutely fine. No, I'm not upset. No, but I'm not telling you the next story. You can tell the next story. The whole story. A proper story. Come on. I'm waiting.

So I told the next story, and as it unfolded I realized how exciting it could be to know more about a story than you knew. I hadn't really understood how exhilarating it could be to hold your attention like that.

The end, I said.

But that can't be the end, you said. Were they really brother and sister? Why wouldn't he help her? Why couldn't she tell him? How can two people love each other so much but not know it? How can two people love and hate each other so much at the same time? How can two people have so much experience in common, and then nothing? What happened when they got older? Did they see each other? Did it ever stop being like that?

You rolled over when you thought I was asleep, and I could feel you next to me, biting on your fingernails, wondering about the people in the story. To me there was no mystery; the characters were just characters I had made up to intrigue you, and although I had enjoyed it, now, lying next to you and sensing your mind elsewhere, I wished I had the luxury of wondering about them too.

You tell the next story, I said in your ear. Please.

No, you, you said. *You* tell it.

But I can be persuasive, and we were sitting up, leaning on each other in the early morning light; now that it was May the light came in just before three and soon there would be almost no dark at all. Birds sang and leaves lifted, and the door to your bedroom was always open because all the doors in the house warped in the summer. You leaned back, and began a story; there was once, you said, someone who was in love with the sky.

Yes, I said, and I could see the sky spread out before her as she ran towards it with her arms out, a never-ending blue, travelling steadily round the world with the weather racing below it, nothing above the clouds but light. I held your hand and closed my eyes. I imagined her saving her money so she could go up in planes and jump out of them, free-falling through the empty air. She loves the sky, I thought, because it's the one thing in life that will always be there, that will never go away. She probably loves trees too, and puts her arms around them in the park to speak to all the years ringed into their trunks.

You were still talking. And so, in the end, you were saying, his mother gave in and saw how good it all was and stopped being ashamed and let them live together, so they got a flat in London and settled down and were happy ever after. The end.

Who settled down? I said. Who lived together? I don't get it. How could you settle down in a flat with the sky?

You looked hard at me as if I was mad.

Unless she lived in a top flat, did she? I said. And she put in dormer windows. So she could see it above her all the time.

Your mouth fell open and you looked at me as if I was speaking in a language you couldn't understand. I was frightened. I couldn't think why you were looking at me like this. But you burst out laughing. Not the sky, you said. Not the sky. There was once a man who was in love with *this guy*.

You teased me about it until we lay exhausted with laughing, the covers thrown off on to the floor now because of the heat. You're so unromantic, I said. I told you my version of the sky story. You're too romantic, you told me. It was July and the air in the room was still, weighted and scented with deep summer. I watched a bead of sweat as it ran down between your shoulders, felt sweat laze down my neck and settle in the hollow of my own collarbone, and then it was September and the air crisper and cooler, I leaned down and pulled the covers back on.

You told the story of the man who blows up a building because he is in love with a film star he can't have, and the one about the people who love and adore a statue so much that they cover its feet in flowers; the story of the teacher so in love with a girl in her class that she writes poems about it and publishes them in magazines, and the one about the god who spends eternity tending a broken egg. I can't remember what stories I told. We took turns to tell, one line each, the story of the person who has fallen in love with his or her own reflection, who finds a basic kind of love, as you called it, in every shop window.

It was cold. We were both tired. We got into bed because the heating had switched off and we were trying to save money by not switching it on again after half-past ten. You rolled into my arms. I put my cold feet on your shins to warm them up.

Tell me a story, you said.

Okay, I said. Any particular kind of story?

A love story, you said.

So I huddled in the slow-warming bed. I lay with your head on my arm and I tried to think of how to put it. I thought about how I cycled round town these days wearing a shirt you used to wear ten years ago, when I first knew you. But I didn't want to tell you this; it was a thing of private pleasure to me. I thought how much I liked the way you open a door and stand in the doorway, leaning on the frame. But I thought if I told you about it, it might stop you doing it. I thought how like a great cat you were, padding through the rooms of our house and towering your shoulders over me at night. But I didn't want you to know I thought this; it was something I liked to think only I knew about you. I thought of your voice in the dark. When I had first heard your voice like that I had known that I would love you.

But that's not what I said.

There was once, I said, a story that was told by way of other stories. The end.

You didn't say anything. I whispered in your ear. Will that do? I said.

I heard you speak from somewhere near sleep.
That'll do, you said.

Your warm hand traced down the path of my spine and rested on my groin. My arm went across your shoulders, held the covers up round your neck. It was November, and a year was ending again and another one coming round.

Goodnight, we said, like every night, and you longingly hopelessly happily fearfully selfishly loyally temptingly knowingly passionately lovingly wordlessly kissed me

and I kissed you all of it back

goodnight.